Upon A Fine Horse

UPON A FINE HORSE

William Cates

Calavira Publishing
Los Olivos, California

UPON A FINE HORSE
by William Cates

ISBN 978-1-936214-51-8

Library of Congress Control Number: 2011932540

©2011 by William W. Cates

All rights reserved. No part of this book may be used or reproduced by any means without written permission from the publisher except in the case of brief quotations embodied in critical articles and reviews.

Ilustrations by Gwen Cates

Calavira Publishing, Imprint of Wyatt-MacKenzie
Calavira, LLC
P.O. Box 594
Los Olivos, California 93441

www.calavira.com

This is a work of fiction. All the characters, names, incidents, organizations and dialogue in this book are either the products of the author's imagination or are used fictitiously.

To Gwendolyn

The Riding Master's Lesson
1

The Challenge Trail
25

The Wrong Bit
41

Dancing With Desiree
49

Midnight's Sidekick
75

The Best Motel In Town
89

Stonewall Jackson's Saddle
105

The Lodge
119

Flowers For Miz Bonny
139

WILLIAM CATES

The Riding Master's Lesson

Horses. Girls love them. I love them, too, but not in the same way girls do. For me riding is a sport, it's seeing the countryside from a horse's back. For girls, riding a horse is controlling a big, handsome animal with hands and heels, having the reins in their fingers and twelve hundred pounds of muscle and bone between their legs, and being on top.

How do I know this? Direct experience. For starters, there was Lisa Lockett Elsmendorf who came to the riding stable where I sometimes worked. She was already a pretty good rider as far as balance was concerned. Like me, she had done some bareback riding, but unlike me, she often rode naked. At least that's what she told me.

Lockett's family had an orchard further out the road from the riding stable, the Elsmendorf Orchards. They were well known for their apples, and they made a big deal over the fact that they never sprayed their orchards to kill the bugs. They said they invited birds and helpful insects in to eat the bad insects. My mom considered them weird people. Still, she bought their apples even though we sometimes found worms in them.

At school Lockett went her own way never mixing with the other kids. She wasn't snooty, her head was just somewhere else. Of course the other students made unfriendly comments about her since she was so hard to get to know. But nobody crossed her and for good reason: she wore badges and pins on her jacket displaying her marksmanship awards. I figured she was good with a gun because she was so steady and calm, and when she looked at me it was like she was taking aim.

The day she showed up at the stable, we recognized one another, so we struck up a conversation. She was a year ahead of me in school and we had no classes together, but we had noticed each other in the hallway and cafeteria. I always smiled at her because she was nice-looking and always alone with an expression like she was searching for something way far off in the distance. She had reddish-brown hair and eyes the color of a bullet. I could tell that being a cheerleader or majorette was not for her, even though she had more going for her than a lot of the girls who bounced along the sidelines of the football field or pranced ahead of the marching band.

One day after her riding lesson, Lockett walked into the stall where I was unsaddling the horse she had ridden. When I lifted the saddle off the horse, she told me she usually rode bareback with only a small saddle pad. "Saddles separate you from the horse," she said, putting her hand on the horse's withers and slowly sliding her hand along the horse's back. "I want to feel the horse's muscles flexing between my legs, feel the beat of his heart, the heat of his body, and the soft hair against my skin. And when the weather is warm, I don't wear clothes at all when I ride. I want to be one with the horse, canter through our orchards feeling the full force of nature caressing my skin."

I didn't know what to say for a moment. But I was beginning to see why she didn't talk to the other kids at school. Finally I managed, "Suppose somebody sees you?"

"So somebody sees me. So what?"

"Wouldn't that be uh ..."

"Why should it?" she answered like she was correcting me for asking.

"I don't know. What about bugs biting you in places you don't want to be seen scratching?"

"We don't have pesky bugs at our farm because we have birds to take care of that problem."

"Birds. Yes, of course." I gave a little bird whistle.

Lockett laughed. "Very cute," she said. She kissed the horse on the neck, squeezed out a little smile for me and left the stall.

That was our first conversation. The next time she came for a lesson, I watched her ride (even though she had her clothes on) just to see if she pulled her legs back and tilted forward the way the Indians in western movies rode. And she did, but the riding master was calling out to her, correcting her posture.

"Back straight, heels down. Hip, shoulder, and heels in a straight line," he was telling her as she trotted her horse around the arena.

Lockett drove her own car, so when she finished riding she didn't hang around the stable waiting for a ride like some of the other girls. I always hoped she would stay until I finished work so I could get to know her better. One day she did stay. She was heading for her car after her riding lesson but turned around and came back into the stable and asked if she could help me do anything.

This sudden friendliness took me by surprise. I didn't know what to say until I managed to mumble, "Sure."

"I like you," she offered. "You're one of the nicest boys at school."

"But we've never even spoken at school."

"Yes, but you always look at me and smile. A smile goes a long way."

"I guess so. Well, I just have to finish cleaning the tack. You can help me with that."

"Tell me what to do."

So I gave her a sponge and a bar of glycerine saddle soap and together we soaped up the rest of the saddles, then wiped them down. While we worked, she asked me if I liked the school.

"It's okay. I don't have anything to compare it with. I've had a few really good teachers, like Mr. Lemon. He makes history come alive when he stalks around in front of the class waving a sword and acting out Virginia history—you know, playing Lee surrendering to Grant or Cornwallis surrendering to Washington."

"Yes, I took his class, too, and I hope you remembered what he said about not trusting history books, because they don't always tell it the way it really happened. When we studied the Revolutionary War he told us Cornwallis did not hand his sword over to Washington the way the history books show. Cornwallis refused to get out of bed the day the British surrendered."

"Some days it's really tough to get going."

"But not when you're representing an entire country."

"Guess so."

"Too bad everyone makes fun of Mr. Lemon's name and the fact that he looks so sour. But names can make their own statement. And by the way, please call me

Lockett, not Lisa."

The riding master called her Lisa and I think the teachers at school called her Lisa. I had actually never called her anything.

"Lisa is okay, but it says nothing about me," she said. "I'm going to be a freethinker. And Lockett is better."

"A freethinker? Thinking is already free."

"No. It means I won't accept beliefs or other people's opinions. I want to discover facts for myself and come to my own conclusions about everything."

"I think that's a good idea," I told her.

"Ah, you're accepting my opinion."

"I am?"

"You agreed with me, didn't you?"

"But there's nothing wrong with agreeing with you if you're right."

"That's a good point. But you still need to look at everything and draw your own conclusions."

"Can I look at you riding without your clothes on? And draw a conclusion?"

"If you want to."

"I'm thinking I want to be a freethinker. Probably a good way to get started."

"You're funny." Then she told me she would get her own horse out that afternoon at 4:00 and ride through their orchard. "You can watch me then if you want to."

"I'll be there." And I was. At 3:30 I rode my bike all the way over to the Elsmendorf's orchard and waited. I leaned my bike against an apple tree and wandered around the orchard until I heard hoof beats. And sure enough along came Lockett without a stitch on, cantering down between the rows of apple trees. She didn't wave or even look at me but rode on by like I wasn't even there. It was like she was riding in her sleep. I watched until she was out of sight. I stayed a while in case she rode back but she didn't. What a sight! It was weeks before I saw anything to compare with it. But thanks to Lockett, I was beginning to see the possibilities in freethinking.

The next time Lockett came for a riding lesson, I told her I had seen her ride naked in the orchard and that I had looked at the facts and formed my own opinion. "No matter what other people might believe, a naked girl on a horse is about as pretty a sight as this world has to offer," I told her.

Instead of responding to my comment, she said, "How would you like to have a girth pulled tight around your tummy and a saddle rubbing your back?" She was wearing a jacket with a bunch of marksmanship badges sewed onto it. That kind of distracted me.

"I wouldn't even want a bit in my mouth," I finally managed to tell her.

But whoa. I'm getting ahead of myself. I'll get back to Lockett later. I need to explain about this riding school and how I got my job there.

When I was in high school my folks bought a house just on the edge of the town of Weyridge, Virginia. Beyond our place it was mostly woods except for a dairy farm and a few frame houses with big gardens and lots of roaming chickens. It was pretty country, this broad valley surrounded by mountains hazy in the distance. Further out the road from our house was a riding stable, an easy ride on my bike. One Saturday when I was riding by the stable I stopped, parked my bike and watched a horse going over a course of jumps. There was a woman on the horse's back and a man standing out in the middle of the riding arena giving her instructions and changing the height of the jump poles. When she finished her ride and was heading for the exit gate, the man walked over to the fence rail I was leaning on and asked me if I rode horses.

"Yes Sir," I said. "Every chance I get." (which was some bareback riding on a friend's horse.)

"I could use another good man," he said. He had an English accent and looked kind of starchy. "Would you know of anyone?"

That's how it all started. I'd just gotten my driver's license and needed to make some money so I could buy a car. I also wanted to be a "good man." So I took this Saturday job working for the riding master. And my world changed.

He let me ride some of his horses and he taught me to sit up straight in the saddle, elbows down, hands steady, head up, heels down. "You shall ride like a gentleman. Think of your reins as silk ribbons," he said. "And we do not get our balance from silk ribbons. Or the horse's mane."

It didn't take me long to figure out that this riding school was a good place to be. Girls outnumbered guys twelve to one, and half those guys weren't interested in girls. The riding master told me I had good balance, good hands. He said I was a natural. I could be a top rider if I worked at it. I guess he meant it.

So there I was every Saturday morning, mucking stalls, grooming and saddling horses. Before the students showed up, the riding master marched into the stable to inspect the horses the other two stable hands and I were saddling up. After a walk around each horse making sure their coats were brushed to a fine shine and there was no trace of bedding straw left in their tails, he would slip three fingers under the horse's girth at the buckle and slide his hand to the horse's belly checking tightness. He eyed the bridle and checked the curb chain, and adjusted it for each particular horse. When he was satisfied that the horse was ready for his students, he gave a little nod, clicked his heels together and marched on to the next stall.

In a little while the stable filled with girls, all wearing tight riding breeches and jodhpur boots and twirling riding crops in their fingers. Nearly half tied their hair in ponytails. A few mothers trailed along with their daughters. The riding master, looking gallant and sporty, greeted them at the doorway of his stable, flashing his white teeth and calling each rider by the correct name. If one of the mothers began fishing into her purse he was quick to offer her a cigarette from his gold plated cigarette case. He had a lighter ready. ("A woman loses eighty percent of her sexuality if she lights her own cigarette," he explained to me.) Watching a woman cock her head back and lock her eyes with his while exhaling that first puff of smoke made me eager to learn their secret silent language.

The riding master's name was Mr. Neils Hamlyn and he always dressed in riding breeches with high leather boots, a tan dress shirt with gold plated cuff links and a tie, even if he wasn't planning to ride. "One's attire prepares one mentally and emotionally for the correct approach to good horsemanship," he explained. I soon realized that what he really wanted was to look his best for the mothers who camped along the fence rail watching their kids develop into riders. And for the women who took riding lessons from him.

When he did ride, he looked nifty on a horse the way short men do. It's the proportions, the tight compact body proudly erect in the saddle. I could tell from their almost smiles that the women standing at the fence rail enjoyed watching him ride. With my long legs I'd never look as good as he did.

When school ended for the summer, my Saturday job at the stable turned into a full time job. I should give the place its proper name: Elysian Fields Equestrian Center. That sounded a lot better than the place my dad wanted me to work—Wordstrum's Wood Products, a lumberyard a friend of his owned. "Jack Wordstrum's got it made. He can't fill the demand for lumber with all the building that's going on around here. Lumber is the future, not those damned horses." My dad and I didn't get along. He told me I wasn't a team player and I'd never amount to anything unless I learned to fit in. He had no use for horses. "A waste of time and money," he'd say. Boxing was his sport. And cockfights. Obviously, we didn't see eye to eye on many things, but like Mr. Hamlyn told me, "People who see eye to eye only see each other's eyes." I didn't look anything like my dad and sometimes wondered if he really had fathered me. Maybe he wondered about that, too. He was big and heavyset with dark hair and brown eyes. Maybe I got all of my mom's genes. She looked like me—fair-haired with blue eyes. And no matter how much we ate, we never put on a pound, unlike my dad.

Mr. Hamlyn and his wife, Felicia, owned Elysian Fields Equestrian Center. My mom told me she had heard at church that the farm really belonged to Felicia's father who bought it for his daughter as a wedding gift, hoping a bit of real earth might ground her. But even I could see there was no way to ground that woman. She enjoyed riding but I always had the feeling she was late for something that offered bigger thrills and a lot more pleasure. She would send word to the stable which horse she wanted me to saddle for her, dash from the house to the stable and mount up without ever once looking at me, even though I was holding her horse for her. All the other women who rode looked at me and smiled. One woman even slipped a fifty-cent piece into my hand just for leading her horse to the mounting block and holding it for her when she mounted.

Mrs. Hamlyn would take off toward the back hay field at a gallop. She'd be back in half an hour with the horse in a lather, jump off and toss the reins to me, and be gone. I heard she had an apartment in New York, so I guess that's why she was rarely around the farm.

Tuesdays, Thursdays, and Sundays were the days Mr. Hamlyn rode. Those were the days one of the adult female riders would show up for lessons or for a trail ride. He usually rode a horse he called Awesome Rex. Rex was a big boned liver chestnut with three white stockings and a white star on his forehead. He was seventeen hands tall, a handsome horse with a long neck and good slope to his shoulders.

"Saved this horse from the *knackers*," Mr. Hamlyn announced as I was getting Rex ready for him.

I had Rex in the crossties when Mr. Hamlyn walked into the stall for his inspection. I wasn't sure what *knackers* meant but I thought it had something to do with the glue factory (and it does).

Mr. Hamlyn stood back admiring Rex. "Brought him home from the stockyard for the price of gasoline going and coming."

I turned and looked at Mr. Hamlyn waiting for an explanation.

"The horse was wild. He had gotten away from the farmer who brought him to the stockyard, slipped his halter and was running loose all over the place. And nobody could lay a hand on him. A bunch of buckaroos in bib overalls were chasing him, trying to lasso the horse. And this fine fellow here, he was leaping and bucking and kicking out at anybody who got near him. Finally, the farmer said 'Anyone who can catch that crazy son-of-a-bitch can have him.' Well, there I was standing on the other side of a six-foot tall board fence watching the action. Finally, some men got the horse cornered up against the fence but they just stood there, the men eyeing the horse and this horse, his eyes nearly popping out of his head, eyeing the men. His nostrils were flaring like a dragon and his hooves striking out at them and none of those men daring to make another move."

Looking at Rex standing quietly in the crossties while I brushed him, it was hard for me to believe Mr. Hamlyn was talking about the same horse. "So what did you do?"

"Well a horse only thinks of one thing at a time, so I pulled out my handkerchief, tied it in a loop, climbed up on the fence, leaned way over, dropped it onto his ear and pulled it tight. This horse just stood frozen, paralyzed, his eye turned to look up at his ear trying to figure what was going on. So then I pulled off my belt, put it around his neck and climbed over the fence and led him like a dog over to my truck and loaded him up. 'Sorry gentlemen,' I said to those men standing there with their mouths hanging open, 'But this one's mine.' There must have been a half-dozen farmers looking like they had just seen Houdini halter a rhino."

I think he told me that story to give me confidence, a kind of horse parable. If nothing else worked with a wild and crazy horse, I knew I could always pull out a handkerchief and tie it around the horse's ear. From that day on I started carrying a handkerchief, even after I learned the story wasn't true.

One day I was standing at the fence rail beside Mr. Hamlyn as we watched one of his advanced riders, Mrs. Durrington, take a course of jumps he had set up for her. I had saddled her horse and helped her mount up and stayed to see how the horse was going. Mr. Hamlyn pulled out a cigarette, lit it and gestured toward Mrs. Durrington. "You've got to like a woman with a figure like that." I hadn't paid that much attention to her figure, but Mr. Hamlyn was all smiles as he watched her horse clearing the jump going away from us. "Yes, quite a good seat," he said. I thought I could hear his teeth click.

Mrs. Durrington had a daughter, Becky, who also rode at the farm when she wasn't playing tennis (which was most of the time). Maybe he was thinking about Becky and her mom when he told me, "A woman with a teenage daughter is the most restless woman you will ever encounter. By that time, the mother is bored with her husband and whether she knows it or not, she's in competition with her daughter... and is accustomed to winning." Then he said, "Never turn down an opportunity to understand a woman's need for attention."

I was pleased that he had taken me into his manly confidence although I didn't really know what he meant by some of that advice. A few weeks later, I understood.

Some afternoons after classes had finished, I would see him disappear into the farm office with one of the mothers who drove back to the farm after dropping her daughter off at the country club. Or it might be one of the women who stayed after her riding lesson.

The farm office was a small, stand-alone cabin about twenty yards from the stable. Made of logs, it had been the first structure built on the farm and dated back to the late 1700s. Mr. Hamlyn had it moved from a hill above the creek to a more useful location next to one of the paddocks behind the stable where it was shaded by a huge oak tree. "Eighty percent of the sun's heat is absorbed by the leaves of this tree," he told me. The office did stay cool even on the hottest days of summer. He had placed a sign over the door that read, *There is Nothing so Good for the Inside of a Man as the Outside of a Horse.*

Moggins Barlow did most of the real work at the stable, seeing that the horses were fed morning and evening, their stalls were clean, and the tack kept in spotless condition. In fact, Barlow looked after the entire farming operations, even getting up hay in the summer. Moggins, according to Mr. Hamlyn, was a decorated war veteran. The war had left Moggins with a bad limp, but as Mr. Hamlyn said, Moggins could, when sober, do the work of three good men. Moggins did keep a pint of bourbon in the feed room tucked under sacks of oats. Some days he hit it pretty heavily and started saying things he normally wouldn't say, like telling me Mr. Hamlyn didn't get Awesome Rex from the stockyard, but that the horse belonged to a customer who had been boarding the horse and skipped out without paying the board bill. And it was Moggins who clued me in on the activities that went on in the office.

"You don't think he goes in there and just talks to them," Moggins told me one day as we led horses out to the paddocks to graze. Mr. Hamlyn had disappeared into the office with a woman I only got a glimpse of. I didn't know how to respond to comments like that so I just shook my head and gave Moggins Barlow a man-to-man smile of understanding. Maybe I thought they'd have a drink and smoke a few cigarettes and talk about the horses.

Late one afternoon, long after the riding lessons were over and the horses turned out to pasture, I was leading one of the mares out to turn her loose to graze with the other mares in the paddock behind the office. The mare had thrown a shoe during the last class and we had left her in the stall until Moggins had time to tack it back on well enough to hold until the next visit from the farrier. Nearing the gate to the paddock, I heard a woman's voice making a sound I had never heard, and a man's soft laughter coming from the open window at the back of the office.

"Listen to you. Just listen to you," I could hear the man's voice saying.

After I slipped the halter off the horse and stepped back through the open gate and latched it, I snuck over to the open window and peered in.

There on a sofa lay Mr. Hamlyn with Mrs. Durrington riding him like she was going at a full gallop. He still wore his shirt though it was unbuttoned and falling open and his riding breeches were pulled down around his ankles, and Mrs. Durrington was naked except for her neck scarf. Her blouse was dangling off one of Mr. Hamlyn's riding boots that was resting next to a bottle of bourbon. Mr. Hamlyn was definitely satisfying her need for attention (and she was satisfying his).

Until that moment, I had seen the office as a sacred equestrian shrine. The walls were covered with framed black and white photos of some of the greats of the horse world along with famed horsemen of the Confederacy (In the south, the Civil War was about character not issues. Lee was a gentleman, Grant a drunkard.) Man o' War, Citation, Sea Biscuit, Dan Patch and Greyhound hung across the room from pictures of Robert E. Lee on Traveler and Stonewall Jackson astride Little Sorrel. JEB Stuart, John Mosby, and others had their place of honor in this small room furnished with a roll top desk, a liquor cabinet (kept under lock and key), several chairs, a wood burning stove and a large comfortable sofa covered with soft leather.

During rainstorms Mr. Hamlyn moved his classes into the office. Students would sit on that very same sofa or on the floor on a rug he rolled out from under the sofa. In cold wet weather he would build a fire in the woodstove connected to a sealed-over fireplace. He was a great storyteller, especially with that English accent; he could draw on a wealth of horse stories that would eventually lead to how saddles evolved or how to choose the correct bit for your horse. The office was a place of honor and learning.

Yet there they were under the gaze of the Confederate military command, huffing and puffing and laughing and groaning. I had seen dogs and cows and horses having sex, none of it appealing—although a stallion standing at his full height on his hind legs with that enormous erection is pretty impressive. I had never really thought about how humans would look (and sound). The scene was riveting, but not what I had expected. Seeing Mrs. Durrington in all her glory aroused me, but seeing so much of Mr. Hamlyn's very white skin and skinny legs was like seeing how a magician does his tricks. Without his clothes Mr. Hamlyn wasn't the riding master. I didn't know who he was. I crept away from the open window holding my breath.

Another of Mr. Hamlyn's favorites was Mrs. Rhodes. Her husband owned the local Pontiac dealership, giving her access to new and used cars off the lot. On a bright sunny day you could count on her breezing into the parking area at the wheel of a convertible. Whatever she drove she advertised beautifully and I would have settled for any of those cars. Mrs. Rhodes had bright red hair that she tried to keep down with a scarf but it billowed behind her like a burning bush.

Mrs. Rhodes was a saddle seat rider and with her flashy looks she was perfect for the showy saddle seat role. *Nouveau riche* of the horse world, Mr. Hamlyn called them. Mr. Hamlyn leaned toward hunt seat but Elysian Fields Equestrian Center was one of those rare riding stables where both riding styles were taught and enjoyed.

Luckily, Mr. Hamlyn had found an over-the-hill five-gaited saddle horse at the Tattersalls auctions in Kentucky that was the perfect mount for Mrs. Rhodes. This horse, Denmark's Royal Big Time Chief, had a fancy name and style to go with it. Though the horse was about fifteen years old and finished in the show ring, he still had some get up and go. Occasionally Mrs. Rhodes put the horse through all five gaits with the horse trotting and racking with the speed of a racehorse around the arena, and Mrs. Rhodes sitting back in the saddle making it look like it was as easy as driving a new Pontiac. I think that horse could move on under saddle as fast as a trotter or pacer on the track pulling a racing bike. Mrs. Rhodes also took the horse on the trail when riding with Mr. Hamlyn. When they returned, I would take their horses so they could go to his office for a drink before she headed home, an hour or so later.

Mrs. Lauren DuBeer was another rider he spent a lot of time with. She and her husband ran an accounting firm, and according to Mr. Hamlyn, she needed to get outdoors and away from numbers from time to time. He told me she was one of the top accountants anywhere around. The DuBeers had no children; they focused their lives on their work. Her husband had no use for horses. Golf was his sport. That was convenient for Mr. Hamlyn.

I enjoyed watching Mrs. DuBeer ride because not only did she have a good seat, she seemed up for any challenge. Mr. Hamlyn could set the jumps at three and half feet and she would laugh and motion to him to go higher. Archery was her second sport, Mr. Hamlyn told me. It was easy for me to picture her standing in the stirrups drawing a bow while galloping full speed at some target.

There were other women who came and went, but these three women got most of his attention. Not only was he able to charm women, he could also juggle several relationships at one time. And he was discreet. According to Moggins, only once did a jealous husband show up to settle the score. It was Mr. Rhodes. He rolled up in one of his new Pontiacs and stormed into the barn with a gun in his hand. But Moggins told him that Mr. Hamlyn wasn't around that day, and even if he was, he wasn't worth shooting. They had a drink together and Rhodes went back to sell some more Pontiacs.

Mr. Hamlyn made it clear to me there was a difference between women and girls and I had better respect that distinction. Women were fair game, especially married women because if they got pregnant they had husbands to thank. Girls, his riding students, were off limits. I could take a woman out on the trail, or a group of girls, but not a lone girl. Nor could I take a girl alone into the office. Once he pointed to the ladder going up into the hayloft over the stable. "I had better never hear the sound of a zipper being undone in that hayloft with one of my students." Not that he could hear a zipper unzipping from all the way up in the loft, but he got his point across. He must have gotten word from Moggins that I'd been going up into the hayloft with some of the girls and it wasn't to feed the horses.

Sometimes parents dropped off their daughters at the farm for riding lessons and didn't get back until late afternoon to pick them up. After the riding classes were over for the day and the horses turned out into the paddocks and my work was done, I'd wander out into the orchard paddock with one of the girls. The socializing we did in full sunlight was acceptable. It might be Becky or Lydia who would go with me, or some days it was Page, a girl I'd seen my first day at work and couldn't stop thinking about. We would sit shoulder to shoulder under one of the apple trees and talk about the horses.

"Musket Ball's my favorite horse in the whole stable. He's the best," Page would announce thoughtfully while holding an almost ripe apple and staring off into the distance. "And Pancake is my second favorite. I wish I could take them home with me. You're lucky. You get to ride horses every day. And you are never alone when you have a horse."

I couldn't image a girl as pretty as Page being alone for long. We'd talk about the peculiar habits of Storm King and Gypsy Girl or Ginger, how hard it was to get Golddigger to pick up the correct canter lead, or how rough Little Dixie's trot was. It was that sort of thing.

We didn't ride in thunderstorms. When thunder

rumbled and the rain came down in torrents, we put the horse back in the stall and all of the students would go to the office for one of Mr. Hamlyn's lectures. It was the sensible thing to do. The last place you'd want to be in a thunderstorm is out in an open field on a big animal wearing metal shoes.

After Mr. Hamlyn left to go to his house, I might sneak up into the hayloft with one of the girls. We'd lie back on a broken bale of hay and keep talking horses (fortunately those girls never knew we kept a couple of black snakes in the hayloft to help manage the rat population). If thunder rumbled close by, my arms were there for protection. Well, I couldn't ward off lightning, but I could get a girl's mind off the thunder.

Mrs. Durrington's daughter, Becky, wasn't as good a rider as her mother, but she was just as pretty, a slenderer copy. She had full lips and wore bright red lipstick that made them look ripe for kissing. And they were. I know because one rainy day when her mother was late coming to pick her up, I talked her into going up into the hayloft with me. We settled down in the loose hay and listened to rain falling on the tin roof.

"I love it," she said.

"What?"

"The sound of rain on a tin roof. The rhythm. It's so primitive. It reminds me of being at my grandmother's house."

"Yeah. Where does she live?"

"On a farm near Bedford. Way out in the country." She gave a little sigh. "I like going to sleep listening to the patter of rain on a roof."

"Don't go to sleep."

"I'm not, silly."

All the while we talked we inched closer and closer together. Finally we were shoulder to shoulder staring at the cobweb covered ceiling rafters. Then we rolled over facing one another. Becky took her little finger and raked her fingernail across my cheek.

"I like your cheekbones."

"Yeah."

Then she carefully raked her fingernail across my lips.

"You notice the difference?"

"It tickled more on my lips."

"That's because your lips are more sensitive than the rest of you."

"Do it again."

She did and she was right.

"So what's that supposed to mean?"

"It means you're going to be a good lover," she said, closing her eyes and kissing me a long deep kiss. Then she jumped up saying she thought she heard her mother's car coming up the driveway. She couldn't possibly hear a car with the rain beating down on the tin roof of the barn. It was a polite way of saying we'd gone far enough. I couldn't get up. I just lay there in the hay as she climbed down the ladder from the loft. She gave me a quick wave before she disappeared out of sight. When she was gone, my mental snapshot of her mother naked on the sofa in the office popped into my mind. I guess she had warned her daughter about men.

But no zipper was ever unzipped. Only once did a blouse come off and that was to shake the hay out. It was Page who did that. She stood over me while I was lying in the hay, her legs straddling mine as she unbuttoned her blouse, took it off and shook the hay in my face. Then laughed. Every time that scene replayed in my mind, I wish I had been cool enough to yawn rather than goggle at her pointy white bra.

Nothing would ever really happen between us because most of the girls who rode horses lived in the older gentrified part of town, Riggles Creek. They went to Briarwood Country Day School (probably not a haven for freethinkers) and only dated boys from Riggles Creek and their private school. Other than the world of horses, we had no social contact. Around horses there's always a sort of social neutrality but once the girls left the farm for home, even a phone call was out of the question. ("Who? Oh you mean the stable boy?") I figured that Page and the other girls I kissed in the hayloft would offer their charms to some jock from Briarwood Country Day School, making it easy for me to follow Mr. Hamlyn's number one rule.

At the stable, it wasn't that we were equals; it was just that physical distinctions didn't matter as much as how the horses were going. Sometimes when lunch rolled around, Moggins and I would start joking about how much better a barbeque and some French fries would taste than the sandwiches we all brought to work. Curtis and Lewis, the other two guys who worked at the stable, would pick up on it and finally Curtis would say, "Let's go." He was thinking of hopping into his car and all of us heading to Staley's Bar-B-Que, which was out on Highway 41. Then Lewis would say, "Bring me a carryout." Of course Lewis couldn't go to the restaurant with us. We'd completely forgotten he was colored. I guess we should have boycotted the restaurant but it was the same everywhere.

Curtis said that Moggins' wife was colored. She came back from France with him after the war. Moggins told me she was from Algeria. She did some of the cooking and housecleaning for Mr. Hamlyn and a few of the other families in the neighborhood. If the Barlows hadn't been living on the farm, I don't know where they could have lived. Lewis lived in the colored section of town and I guess Moggins and his wife would have lived there, too, since she was darker than any of the white people around.

Not all the girls who rode at the farm lived in Riggles Creek. There was Cheryl Gilwall who lived in a new subdivision down the road and had a quiet little mare she rode out to the farm on one of the trails. She took lessons on her own horse. (More on Cheryl later.)

There were a few more riders from the newer part of town and, as I mentioned, there was Lockett. She had stopped coming for riding lessons. Maybe clothes and a saddle were too much for her. Or maybe she was spending all her spare time on the rifle range. I couldn't stop thinking about her, but I couldn't get up nerve to call her until I saw in the newspaper that a movie called *Rebel Without A Cause* was on at the Garland Theater downtown. From what I'd heard about the movie, I thought it might be Lockett's thing. So, after a half-dozen deep breaths I dialed the Elsmendorf's phone number. I guess it was her mother who answered. I didn't know whether to ask for Lisa or Lockett so I said, "May I speak to Lisa Lockett please?" She asked who was calling and I told her and said I was from the riding stable.

"Just a moment."

When Lockett came on she said, "Hi. Nice of you to call."

I tried for a bit of small talk, which I was never very good at, then finally I asked her if she'd like to go with me to the movies and told her the name of the movie.

"I've already seen it, but I'd like to see it again. It resonated with me."

I had never resonated with a movie but that didn't matter since I was going to be with Lockett.

My mom let me use her car for the evening. I picked Lockett up at her house, which was just past their orchards. What a relief not to have to meet the parents. Maybe they were freethinkers, too, and didn't need to form an opinion about me for this first date with their daughter. Driving downtown Lockett asked me what books I read. I think I had an okay answer with *Treasure Island* but I really hit the mark with *Robinson Crusoe* because she carried on about how Crusoe went against the wishes of his parents and the hardships he went through but how much he grew from his adventures in isolation.

On the way back from the movies we talked about some of the scenes, like the "chicken-run" scene, and why guys feel the need to do that sort of thing.

"Trying to figure what's courage and what's stupidity," I guessed.

She didn't say anything else until we got near her house. Then she said, "Turn down the lane going to the apple sheds."

I gladly did as instructed.

"Over there." She pointed to a graveled parking place on the other side of a tractor. When I cut off the car's engine she said, "Now we can talk." There was a long pause as she glanced out the car window then down at her lap. Finally she said, "I want you to know that I'm going to be leaving next week to drive with my mother to New England to look at colleges and visit with some of her friends and I'm probably going to stay up there until just about time for school to start. So I won't be seeing you anymore except maybe when I come home for school breaks ... if you want to see me."

"Of course I want to see you."

"Good. Have you decided where you want to go to college?"

"I've got a year to think about it, but my mom wants me to go to Cranton-Winsey. She said a lot of doctors and lawyers went there."

"Don't go. You'll hate it."

"Why?"

"I dated a guy who went there. I even visited the school as his guest one weekend. It's all about fraternity parties and getting drunk. They did terrible things to little baby chicks. All the boys I met were so conservative they might as well have been wearing their confederate grays. Discussing anything with them, you realize their education is based on assumption, not observation. Think about it," she said and she reached her hand and touched my face then put her hand behind my neck and pulled me to her. The inside of a car didn't do quite as much for Lockett as the outside of a horse, but we slid down on the seat and got each other's clothes really wrinkled while she gave me my next lesson in free-thinking.

The Challenge Trail

Most of the riding classes were held in the arena. A trail ride was a special reward and taking the riders on the trail became my job. Usually I led about a dozen students out. One day I took only one rider. And she wasn't a young riding student. It was Mrs. DuBeer.

As I mentioned before, not only did Mrs. DuBeer look good on a horse, she looked good just stepping out of her wood decaled Mercury Station Wagon. Walking to the stable, she would put her riding crop between her teeth while tying up her hair. Then she'd stride along smacking her crop against her boots like she was whipping away at some annoying thought lodged in her mind or beating off all those beans she'd been counting.

On this morning I was saddling Musket Ball, getting him ready for the next class, when Mr. Hamlyn hurried into the stall and told me to take Mrs. DuBeer on a trail ride. "A long trail ride," he added looking me hard in the eyes to make sure I understood. "Moggs and Lewis can get the other horses ready. You go! Take my horse if you want."

Mrs. DuBeer had just pulled into the parking area. Through the open window of the stall where I was working, I could see her standing beside her Mercury wagon, tying back her hair, getting ready to ride. Mr. Hamlyn dashed off a note, folded the paper and handed it to me and nodded in her direction. "For her," he said. Then he disappeared.

I don't know if he had overbooked his women friends for the day or if his wife, Felicia, would be making one of her rare appearances at the farm. After Mrs. DuBeer glanced at the note, she tore it into small bits and seeing no trashcan handy, she reached over one of the open stall doors and dropped them into the bedding.

I told her I was instructed to take her out on the trail. She nodded but didn't say a word. I saddled Marigold for her and she led the horse outside while I saddled Awesome Rex for myself. When I led my horse out of the stable, she was standing beside the mounting block but had not gotten on. I wondered if she had changed her mind about riding. "I know some great trails," I told her. I said it like I was promising to sing the national anthem to her.

Mrs. DuBeer forced a smile, mounted up, and we headed out toward the back fields of the farm, the hay fields. Without saying a word, I started my horse trotting off ahead of her because she had a look on her face like she was ready to bite the head off a snake. I didn't even consider a leisurely walk. We rode across the big field at the foot of the mountain before reaching the property line. There was a horse bone yard near the property line and my instructions were to keep that reality out of sight of the trail riders. But Mrs. DuBeer knew about it and rode her horse up to it and stopped and stared down at some of the bones. Maybe she was remembering one of her favorite horses from years past. I kept going and in a few minutes she caught up with me. When we got to the farm property line fence, there was a gate I could open without dismounting. This looked hard to do and always impressed other riders, and I wanted to impress Mrs. DuBeer. I think I did.

We crossed a paved road and picked up a trail that Moggins, Curtis, and I had recently cut through the woods. It was new to Rex and he moved along the trail with his ears up, his eyes searching for an excuse to see something the other horse didn't see and make a big deal over it. I could feel his muscles tensing every time a bird swooped close overhead. Every now and then he would get so worked up over something only he could see, that he'd do a little jig walk like a horse approaching the starting gate at the racetrack. I'd say, "Easy now Rex. Nothing's going to hurt a big fellow like you," and pat him on the neck and he'd settle down. Mrs. DuBeer was on one of the most sensible trail horses in the stable, Marigold, so I knew I could take her anywhere I could get my horse to go, and Marigold would give Awesome Rex comfort and security.

Not too far into the woods the trail forked, a beginner's trail going off to the right and a challenge trail with jumps to the left. It was a new section of trail I'd helped clear. We'd left some logs across the trail stacked up about two and half feet high on the left trail. I had never jumped Rex and had no idea how he would respond but I thought it might put Mrs. DuBeer in a better mood if we had a little excitement. Certainly Rex was big enough to go over the logs. He could almost step over them. So I took the challenge trail. We trotted for a short ways then I moved him into a canter as we approached the first stack of logs. When we got to the jump, Rex skidded to a stop like he'd run up against a barn door. Then he did a standing cow leap over the log. I looked around and saw Mrs. DuBeer had pulled her horse up. She turned Marigold around and trotted back down the trail then turned back in my direction easing her horse into a canter. Horse and rider sailed in perfect form over the log. She gave me a look as if to say – this is the way it's done. The next log we came to, Rex leaped over it like he was jumping over the moon.

"Better," Mrs. DuBeer called out. That was the first word she had said since we left the stable. When I looked around to watch, Mrs. DuBeer had Marigold jumping the logs like a seasoned event horse. I was pleased to see her enjoying the ride.

We entered a big open field grown up with nothing but tall grass and broomsage, a good place for a long canter before the trail narrowed again. So we cantered all the way across the field, Rex cantering easily without wanting to grab the bit and run. Mrs. DuBeer rode Marigold along side of me. Glancing at her, I thought I could see her starting to smile. "Let's do it again," she called out. So we circled around, this time crossing the field at a faster pace, both horses churning up the ground like we were jockeying for the turn into the back-stretch. The gallop across the field was just the right therapy for both of us.

We had slowed to a trot as we rounded an outcropping of rocks overgrown with blackberry vines when we flushed a covey of quail that flew up with a noise like drums beating under a blanket. Rex did a crab-scramble leap to the side, nearly jumping out from under me. When I took hold of him he got mad and dove into the bit shaking his head and bucking so hard I thought my teeth were coming out. Somehow I managed to stay on. Marigold, good steady Marigold, paid no attention to the fluttering birds or Rex's antics.

Mrs. DuBeer laughed. "Nice job, Cowboy," she called out. "You got to ride a wild horse."

"Guess I did."

Even though he cut a shine with me, and I didn't know what he'd do next time something startled him, I wasn't about to turn around and head back to the stable. After that, we kept the horses at a steady trot for a while. Trotting settles a horse and Rex needed settling.

Reaching some hills, we slowed to a walk and followed a deer trail up and over the first hill. The steep and winding trail led down into a narrow valley cut through with a creek sparkling in the sunlight. I let Mrs. DuBeer go ahead on Marigold. The mare was quiet and Rex was still fretting from flushing the covey of quail. Down the slope we went with the horses carefully picking their way, my eyes on Marigold's feet then on her tail, which switched back and forth like she was conducting our descent. Halfway down, Rex stumbled but caught himself. I was leaning back in the saddle throwing my weight on his hind feet, which helped him keep his balance. By the time we got to the bottom, I realized the horse had nearly worn himself out.

We should have ridden at a more leisurely pace on a summer morning, for the horses were already working up a lather and we still had a long trail ahead of us if I was to do my job. I suggested we get off at the creek and let the horses take a break and have a short drink.

Mrs. DuBeer dismounted and led her horse to me. "This looks like a perfect place to bring a lover for a picnic. I bet you bring your girlfriends here all the time." I didn't say anything. She smiled and handed me Marigold's reins to hold. "If you will excuse me a moment," she said. She walked around a dense clump of honeysuckle, apparently to relieve herself.

I got off and led the horses to the edge of the creek and let them have a few swallows of the clear water before they muddied it with their feet. Both horses wanted to play in the water, pawing it and splashing as much as drinking. Guess they were cooling themselves down in their own way. When Mrs. DuBeer came back, her shirttail was hanging out and she didn't bother to tuck it in.

"So what was Neils doing this morning that was so urgent?" she asked me.

"I don't know anything about his plans."

"He promised me we'd do a ride this morning," she said eyeing me as though she suspected I knew more.

"Really, I don't."

She turned away and took a few steps along the creek bank upstream from where the horses had stirred up the water. "Do you mind if I cool off?" she asked, even though she never intended to wait for my answer.

With her back to me, she pulled her shirt off and draped it over the branch of a dogwood tree beside the creek. Then she unsnapped her bra and, and to my surprise, even a second bra and tossed them over her shirt. Turning back to the creek, Mrs. DuBeer bent down to the water and picked up several stones and studied them. "I once found an arrowhead in a creek like this," she said, her words coming as casually as if we were both little kids dipping tadpoles from a mud puddle.

"Arrowheads," I said, dumbly. "Good place for Indians." I glanced up at the hillsides as though there could be a scouting party watching us. What else could I say or do? I watched as she picked up more rocks, examined them, and dropped them back into the water. She reached her hands down and cupped up enough water to pat over her neck and face and again for more scoops of water to drip down her back and chest. Standing there with her head tilted back, eyes closed, wearing only those riding breeches and her knee high riding boots, her wet breasts glistening in the sunlight, her elbows pointed to the sky as she dripped water down her back, Mrs. DuBeer became the first goddess of my life; that image became fixed like a photograph in my mind.

"I hate these damn things on a hot day but you sure as hell can't ride a horse without them," she said, picking up her bras. "I even double up just to make sure I don't stretch anything." Glancing at me, the look on my face must have triggered her next move. "What's the matter? Haven't you ever seen a woman before?"

I couldn't tell her the truth – only in magazines and books and Mrs. Durrington, and Lockett, if she counted. But of course I had never seen anything to compare with the reality of Mrs. DuBeer's wet breasts made even more real sparkling in the bright sunlight.

Instead of putting her bras on, she picked up her shirt and stepped back in my direction, tossing shirt and bras over the saddle of her horse. She took the reins of her horse from my hand then took my free hand and placed it on her breast.

"You've never even touched a woman?"

I couldn't find the words. I couldn't even remember I was a freethinker.

"You have them too. Mine are just larger. And more interesting, I suppose."

Holding her breast that was damp and warm and soft, but firmer than I would have guessed, all I could say was, "Good." It was stupid of me, but I was too flustered to find words. Whether she was having fun at my expense or hoping to educate me, expecting me to tie up the horses for a tumble with her in the grass, taking me up the next step into adulthood, I didn't know. Maybe she was really into freethinking and wanting to form an opinion. The only thing I knew was that I wanted to stay there touching her and hold on to the moment for as long as possible. But I didn't know how. Finally I pulled my handkerchief out of my back pocket and handed it to her. "Not a towel but the best I've got."

"Now that's a real gentleman," she said, taking my handkerchief and patting at the water and perspiration on her chest. She handed my handkerchief back to me along with her shirt to hold while she slipped back into her bras. She tugged her shirt back over her damp skin and stood there eyeing me. "And please call me Logan," she said, leaning forward to give me a light kiss on my cheek. "And thank you for being a good companion. Now if you don't mind, would you please give me a leg up?"

From the horse's back, she studied me for a moment. "Too bad we didn't think to bring a picnic today, Cowboy," she said giving me a smile that left me wondering if I'd missed a freethinking opportunity.

If I had been cool, I would have said, "Maybe another time, Ma'am." But instead, I fumbled for words about the horses being rested and ready to go. I told Mrs. DuBeer to ride on ahead. I'd catch up. She smiled and eased Marigold along the path while I mounted my horse and stood in the stirrups trying to make myself comfortable.

The trail led down a long grade to a lake fed by the creek. We rode around the lake with both of us eyeing the clear blue water under the hot midday sun. It was getting so hot I could see wavy lines of heat radiating off the grassy field ahead of us. The water looked more and more inviting as we closed the long loop around the lake. There weren't any houses in sight, and only some rowboats tied up at a weather beaten dock so it was a good place for skinny-dipping, but I didn't have the nerve to suggest it. We rode up to a cove where the creek entered the lake and stopped the horses beneath a big sycamore that spread its limbs far out, offering some much-needed shade.

I stopped my horse and pointed up at the mistletoe. "Did you know that's a sign of underground water – sycamores and mistletoe?"

Mrs. DuBeer looked up at the mistletoe for a long moment. Then she said, "Water. I wish we'd brought a canteen. I'm getting thirsty."

"Me too."

She glanced up into the tree then out across the lake. "Can you swim, Cowboy?"

"Yes Ma'am, I can. I swim a lot."

"Will the horses tie up?"

"They're tired. I think they will."

She swung out of the saddle and I did the same. "You don't mind skinny dipping with an old woman do you?"

"You're not old."

"It's going to be hard getting these boots back on once my feet get wet, but they're sweaty wet already. Hey, we're not on any schedule today are we?"

"No Ma'am."

I reached for Marigold's reins and led the horses over to a smaller tree where I could tie them up. I unfastened the buckle on the reins and looped the reins around the tree just above a low limb and re-buckled them. Then I ran the stirrup leathers up and loosened each horse's girth. Using the reins wasn't the best way to tie the horses but the only way available. These horses weren't like those docile horses in western movies where the rider flips the reins around the hitching post rail as he ambles toward the saloon. I didn't want to chance breaking the reins and letting the horses get away, but I wasn't going to pass up an opportunity to swim with Mrs. DuBeer.

When I turned back, Mrs. DuBeer already had her shirt off and had stretched it out in the sun to dry. She was sitting in the tall grass tugging at her riding boots.

"Can you give me a hand?" she asked, sticking her boot up in the air.

I helped pull her boots off then sat down beside her to tug at mine.

"Need a hand?" she said.

"I can manage."

Before I could get my boots off she was completely stripped and heading for the water. A redwing blackbird flew up out of the cattails at the edge of the lake and into the tree above the horses where it sat fussing at us. Mrs. DuBeer waded past the clump of cattails and stood at the water's edge shaking out her hair.

"Perfect," she called out breaking into the stillness of the water. "A cute little snake right here in the shallows," she added.

"They can't bite under water. At least I don't think they can."

I didn't hear what she said as she waded further out, her body sending slow ripples across the still surface of the lake.

I watched the water rise up the back of her calves, her thighs, her hips. Seeing her, smelling honeysuckle and sassafras, and the earth itself and hearing the music of a hundred insects, I knew then that I would always worship women. When Mrs. DuBeer was in up to her shoulders, she turned back catching me just as I was coming out of my shorts. Well, there was no way to hide my excitement from her. I tried conjugating Latin verbs but nothing was going to work. I turned my back to her and pretended to be watching the blackbird up in the tree. I stepped backwards to the water and waded in. When I turned around, Mrs. DuBeer was smiling as though she fully understood the situation and that it was as much a part of nature as the chattering blackbird and chorus of insects, and it was all just fine. She turned and swam a few yards further out and rolled onto her back and floated, her nose, chin and nipples rising above the surface.

The water was perfect, warm near the surface and cool down around my legs. I was swimming toward Mrs. DuBeer when I saw her point to the horses. I turned around to see Awesome Rex pulling back on his reins. He gave his head a jerk and snapped the leather, then trotted off a short way. He stopped and looked back to see why

Marigold wasn't joining him. But good Marigold stood quietly tied to the tree, lost in her own horse world. Awesome Rex dropped his head and started grazing.

I swam back to shore, and grabbed my boots and managed to get my wet muddy feet into them. A horse usually won't run off and leave another horse, but I was afraid Marigold might get the same idea of freedom in her sweet head and pull loose. It would be a long hot walk back. Besides, how could I catch awesome Rex without her help? So I unfastened Marigold's reins and led her over to where Awesome Rex was browsing. He lifted his head as though hearing some distant call and trotted further off, his reins dragging the ground. I was afraid he was ready to answer whatever he was hearing and race off, maybe all the way back to the stable. I spoke to him with the most soothing, calmest voice I could muster. He looked back at Marigold like he was trying to tell her it was time to romp. Bless her, she wasn't interested or maybe just too tired. I led her closer to him and instead of turning to trot away, he reached out to touch his nose to Marigold's. When he did, I grabbed his dangling reins. Fortunately, they had only snapped at the buckle. I patted Rex and told him everything was okay. Then I led both horses back over to our clothes and stood there, tempted to tie my handkerchief around Rex's ear. Maybe he'd stand still while I got back in the water. But when I pictured him galloping away rider-less with a wet handkerchief tied around his ear, I decided to hold onto what I had.

Mrs. DuBeer was still out in the lake treading water. "Cowboy, I wish I had a movie camera," she called out.

"I'm glad you don't. I just wish I had a good piece of rope to tie them with." I guess it was a sight: the stable boy wearing only riding boots, holding two horses saddled, bridled and ready to ride.

Mrs. DuBeer swam to shore and waded out of the

water. "This is something I'll never forget," she said, walking towards me, wringing water from her hair.

"Me either."

We both stood there in the tall grass, wet, naked and gleaming in the sunlight. I was aching to drop the horses' reins and put my arms around her. But I didn't.

"You can take my shirt and dry yourself," I offered.

She shook the water from her arms and hands. "You are, indeed, a gentleman," she said. "And I'm going to take you up on it."

It was months before I put that pale blue short-sleeved cotton shirt into the laundry basket.

I held the horses while she dressed, then she held them for me. Once we were dressed we looked at one another and started laughing. I tightened the girths and we were ready to ride again.

"Give me a leg up, Cowboy," she said. I did. Then I mounted Awesome Rex and we rode slowly back to the stable, walking all the way. And we talked.

If seeing Mr. Hamlyn half out of his riding master uniform gave me a jolt, it was nothing compared with what Mrs. DuBeer told me on that ride back to the stable. I was always curious to know more about Mr. Hamlyn, so I asked Mrs. DuBeer if he learned to ride in England.

"England? No, I don't think he's ever been to England."

"But he has a British accent."

"Can you keep a secret?"

"I can." (And I did until just now.)

"Neils was born and raised in east Kentucky—coal mining country."

"You're kidding me! I thought he was some English aristocrat."

"He does it well, doesn't he? Actually, he's from a coal mining family. But he didn't dig it, if you'll pardon my pun, so he headed to Lexington hoping to get a job as a jockey. But he was too big, so he got a job as an exercise boy, then he bounced around from racing stables to show jumping and saddle horse stables. Even dressage."

I was speechless. We rode along in silence while I tried to digest what she'd said. "But his accent. How did he ...?"

She smiled and said, "Learned it at the movies."

I stared at her to see if she was kidding me, if she was going to say, "Just joking." But she didn't. "When did you discover he's a fake?"

"Oh no, no, don't say fake." Mrs. DuBeer shook her head. "No, he's for real and smart enough to reinvent himself. Did what he had to do. And pulled off a good act. God knows the world is full of people who would do the same if they had his talent."

"How do you know all this?"

"Partly because I do the taxes for him ... or rather for her."

"His wife?"

"Yes. For the farm. If you know where the money comes from and where it goes you learn a lot about folks. All confidential, of course."

When we got to the newly cut trails, we took the beginners this time. The horses didn't have any jump left in them. And I didn't either. We crossed the paved road and continued on to the gate at the back of the property. I opened it again without dismounting.

"Good job, Cowboy," she said. She headed Marigold across the field toward the pile of horse bones. I followed. When she got there she stopped and looked back at me. "You ever see him with his rifle and his bucket of oats leading an old horse over here?"

"No Ma'am."

"He cries all the way. But he does what has to be done." She turned Marigold toward the stable. "Oh, he's for real in his own way."

Back at the stable there was no one around. Moggins and Curtis had hay to get up and Lewis had gone for the day. I couldn't see if Mr. Hamlyn's car was at his house or not. We unsaddled the horses, turned the hose on them and gulped water from the hose ourselves. We scraped the horses down with the sweat scraper and led them out. Marigold went into the paddock for mares where she trotted across the field to join the other mares standing under a tree, their tails whisking flies off of each other. I turned Awesome Rex out with the geldings. He dropped to the ground and rolled then jumped up, kicking at the sky, then trotted away. He had had a good workout and probably wanted to think about his experience (just as I did).

Mrs. DuBeer stayed to help me clean and put away the tack. She told me she missed that part of the stable experience. We were standing close, side by side, towels in our hands, wiping the lather from the saddles and girths. I kept thinking that Mr. Hamlyn had said consenting married women were fair game. Mrs. DuBeer was married. I wondered if she would consent. I couldn't just ask her and I couldn't picture taking her up to my favorite spot in the hayloft. But I know she was enjoying being with me, having a different kind of afternoon. She even told me I had a good body. Maybe she said it to encourage me. Don't know.

Maybe she just wanted to hang around until Mr. Hamlyn returned so he would see her with her hair curling up around her neck. He'd know she'd been for a swim and she didn't carry a bathing suit on a trail ride. Mrs. DuBeer kept glancing in the direction of the office. Was she wondering if he was in there or was she thinking of us being there? Still time to offer her a drink, I thought, just as he would have done. But I didn't have the key to the liquor cabinet. And suppose Mr. Hamlyn came back and caught us? I was already fretting about an excuse for the broken rein buckle. He had only left instructions for taking her on a long ride. Nothing else. No extra equine entertainment.

Eventually Mrs. DuBeer picked up her riding crop and gave her boot a smack. She stood there for a moment in the middle of the stable isle way as though she didn't know what to do next "Good ride," she said, reaching out and shaking my hand. "I think maybe you're more fun to be with than Neils. I hope we can do it again."

"Me too."

I walked outside the stable with her and watched her head to the parking area. Halfway to her car she started smacking that riding crop against the side of her boot. I guess she had started thinking about counting beans again.

The Wrong Bit

One morning when I got to the stable, there was a small fancy horse van with California license tags parked near the stable. Moggins was backing the manure spreader down the isleway getting ready to clean the stalls. He cut the tractor engine, climbed down and motioned for me to follow him.

"Got something to show you," he said as he limped through to the back door of the stable and out toward a small four-stall barn separated from the main barn. We called it the orchard barn. It was where Mr. Hamlyn kept new horses until he was sure they were healthy enough to mix in with the rest of horses. A place to quarantine them. It also served as a stable where people passing through town could board their horses overnight.

Following Moggins, I thought he had some special horse he wanted me to see. And he did. He limped down to the stall at the end of the stable with me following.

Moggins opened the stall door and stood there with a big grin on his face.

When I looked in there was a black and white pinto bedded down in deep straw and quietly munching away on some hay. The horse raised his head and looked at me with these loco-looking eyes that didn't have much pigment—bluish with a lot of white around the iris. Then he dropped his head and went back to his hay.

"Well?" said Moggins. "You got nothing to say about the horse?"

"Crazy looking eyes."

"Don't you know whose horse it is?"

"You don't see pintos like that around here. Got to be a western horse."

"Okay Dick Tracy, what's the horse's name?"

"How would I know?"

"I bet you do know." Moggins stepped into the stall and patted the horse. "This is the Cisco Kid's horse."

"Diablo!"

"I told you you'd know his name."

"What's the Cisco Kid's horse doing here?"

"They stopped in last night on their way to DC. Puttin' on some kind of show there. An exhibition or something."

"Wow. So this is Diablo."

"This is the traveling Diablo, the guy driving the van told me. They got three of them they use in the movies and on TV. This one knows some stunts, so he gets to go on the road."

"When are they coming to pick him up?"

"I don't know. Sometime this morning I guess."

"I've got to ride him," I told Moggins.

"You can't do that."

"I just want to get on his back for a few minutes so I can say I've ridden Diablo."

"Why don't you clean his stall so you can say you

cleaned up his shit?"

I walked into Diablo's stall and patted the horse. "How about it, Diablo, can I take a quick ride?" Diablo kept munching hay. "Look Moggs, Mr. Hamlyn won't be up here for another hour. He'll never know. "I can find a bridle that ought to fit him. And a saddle."

"I ain't seen nuthin," Moggins said, throwing his hands up in the air. "I got stalls to clean." He lit a cigarette and limped back to the main stable. He'd take as many puffs on it as he could before he got to the barn. Mr. Hamlyn didn't allow smoking inside the stable.

In the tack room, I picked out a simple snaffle bit bridle that would fit just about any horse and grabbed a saddle with a long girth. The pinto was a big-barreled horse. When I put the saddle on his back, the horse turned his head around and looked at it. I guess he'd never had an English saddle on his back. The Cisco Kid had a big western saddle, shiny with silver fittings and edging. It must have weighed three times what the English saddle weighed. Maybe more.

I led Diablo out of the stable, mounted up and rode him around the orchard. I was just going to walk and jog him around, but thinking I'd never have another chance like this, I had to do more. When I got down to the far end of the field, I turned Diablo around heading back towards the stable and put my heels into him. That horse bolted like he'd heard a gunshot and away we went at a full gallop. When I tried to take hold of him it was useless. Hell, the horse was used to a big curb bit, a lot more bit than the snaffle I'd put on him. Diablo paid no attention to that little piece of smooth metal in his mouth. He was full of himself as we raced across the orchard like we were chasing a runaway stagecoach. I couldn't stop him with that bit, but at least I could saw on the bit and guide him in the direction I wanted to go—toward something solid like the wall of the stable. Heading for it at a gallop, he suddenly planted all four feet. His hind feet went underneath him and he almost sat down on his rump as we slid up against the stable wall. One of his stunts, maybe? I hopped off before the horse could get his feet together and make his next move. Taking a good grip of his reins, I thanked Diablo for the ride and neat trick and led him back into his stall.

I had just gotten the saddle and bridle off Diablo when I heard men's voices. Too late to get the saddle and bridle out of the stall, so I buried them under the straw in the dark corner of the stall and kicked some hay over them. Damn good thing it wasn't a western saddle. I could never have hidden it. Well, there I was standing in the stall petting Diablo when Mr. Hamlyn appeared at the stall door with two men I'd never seen before. Actually, one of the men looked a lot like the Cisco Kid, but he was wearing a sports shirt, slacks and loafers rather than a black fancy vaquero outfit with a big sombrero.

"Nice horse," I said.

"Every kid likes to touch Diablo," the man who looked like the Cisco Kid, said with a little bit of a Mexican accent.

They put a halter on Diablo, led him out and loaded him onto the van. The van eased out of the farm driveway with Mr. Renaldo following behind in a car. I should have gotten the Cisco Kid's autograph, but under the circumstances all I could think about was that saddle down in the straw. I also should have gotten somebody to take a picture of me riding Diablo, because when I told Becky Durrington later that morning that I had galloped the Cisco Kid's Diablo in the orchard, she said, "Yeah, right. And I rode Trigger last night before I went to bed."

When the van was out of sight Mr. Hamlyn turned to me and said, "Was he fast?"

"What do you mean?'

"The horse. That pinto. Moved on at a good clip, did he?"

Had he seen me riding the horse? Had Moggins told him? "Which horse?" I asked with all the innocence of a choirboy caught borrowing from the collection plate.

"You know damn good and well what horse I'm talking about! You think I didn't notice that horse's breathing, see his dilated nostrils? A horse doesn't look like that when he's in the stall unless he's colicky or winded."

"I'm sorry, Sir. I just couldn't resist ..."

"You do something like that again and I'll dock you a week's pay."

"Yes sir." If he'd known what Mrs. Dubeer and I had done, I'd probably still owe him money.

Ever since Mrs. DuBeer had told me about Mr. Hamlyn's origins I had been trying to make the truth fit into what I wanted to believe. My first impression of Mr. Hamlyn had been that here was a man of class and distinction, someone I could look up to and admire, unlike my father and the male teachers and coaches at school. Guys look for a male role model and Mr. Hamlyn seemed to have it all. But then he wasn't who he pretended to be. Mrs. DuBeer had called him a re-invented person and insisted he wasn't an imposter, a fake. It was like she was giving him an "A" for his effort to be somebody he wasn't. Maybe I just got hung up on a cheap word like 'fake.' It's easy to do. Everybody lets a few words get in the way of what things really mean. Lockett would probably agree with that. But I was looking for authenticity, the real thing. Finding out about Mr. Hamlyn's act was discouraging. Even the Cisco Kid in slacks, sport shirt, and loafers still had a Mexican accent that was real. But maybe being real didn't matter that much to adults. Maybe we're all actors, I thought.

I've tried playing innocent, tried playing Mr. Cool. Some people just play their roles better than others. Guess it takes practice.

After our long trail ride, Mrs. DuBeer and I always greeted one another with a big hand wave. Either she'd be on a horse or I would. But I never rode with her again. If we passed one another in the stable, she always gave me a smile and asked me how I was doing before hurrying to get on her horse. Late one afternoon, I was in the arena trying out another new horse Mr. Hamlyn had brought in from the stockyard. Mrs. DuBeer was walking from her car to the stable smacking that riding crop against her leg. When she saw me, she stopped to watch me ride. When I trotted my horse close by the rail she called out.

"Hey Cowboy, I heard you got to ride a *real* cowpoke's horse."

"Now where did you hear that?"

"It was all over the news," she said with a grin.

I pulled my horse to a halt, swung around, and we trotted back to the rail beside her. "Well, I did. I rode Diablo and you're the first person who believes me."

"Actually, there's one other," she said, nodding in the direction of the stable. "Hey, when are we going to do that picnic ride?"

"I'm ready whenever you are," I said looking down at her. I thought of how the Cisco Kid would cast a glance at a beautiful senorita standing beside his horse. That kind of stuff comes easy from a horse's back.

"Let's take some rope this time," she said, grinning. "And tie those broncos up."

"Maybe some towels, too," I added.

"What about a picnic basket?"

"Yeah, that, too," I said.

We were both beaming like we'd won the Derby. She actually blew me a kiss and turned to walk to the stable where the riding master in his best hacking attire stood waiting with two horses saddled, bridled, and ready to ride.

Dancing With Desiree

I hated for summer to end. Horseback riding would be limited to weekends or maybe a few hours after school until the days grew too short. On the bright side, there was a new girl at school who caught my eye as soon as I walked through the doorway on the first day of classes. She was standing outside the principal's office holding books under one arm and a classroom chart in the other hand. And frowning.

"You look like you could use some help," I offered. She glanced up at me with a beauty pageant smile. And she could have won first place in my book. "First day here?"

"It is and I am absolutely and completely lost," she drawled with an accent that Vivian Leigh would have admired. "Can you please point me in the direction of room 213B?"

"How about if I just take you there?" (*Miss Scarlett*—I almost added.)

"Why you're just the sweetest thing," she said as we headed down the hallway, with me gallantly introducing myself.

"And I'm Desiree," she replied. "Desiree Duncan."

"Desiree's not a name I've ever heard before."

"It's reserved for special people," she said with a wink.

That wink sealed it. I was smitten. No girl had ever winked at me like that. I have to make an effort to wink, think about squeezing those facial muscles. But she snapped it off as quickly and easily as a camera shutter. And made it look like some special invitation.

So with Desiree at my side, we paraded to room 213B. Heads were turning and the eyes of just about every guy in the hallway did a double take as we passed by. Before leaving her at the classroom door, I checked the rest of her schedule for the day so I could be sure of meeting up with her again, because she was one of the prettiest girls I'd ever seen at Jubal Anderson High School and I was ready to put on my Confederate grays for her, take a class in cotton farming. Whatever it took. Desiree's skin was as pure as porcelain. Seeing her, I couldn't help but think of a China doll my grandmother had on the mantel over her fireplace. Desiree had long brown hair and ocean green eyes and her eyebrows arched like she was in a constant state of pleasant surprise. Maybe she was.

When I caught up with Desiree again after her last class I asked how she liked her teachers.

"Well I don't know yet, Honey," she said. "Give me some time."

Calling somebody you've just met "Honey" caught me by surprise. but coming from her it seemed as genuine and comfortable as my mom's antique rocker.

"I take it you're from the deep south?"

"Well what on earth gave you that idea?" she said, cocking her head to one side and pressing her lips into a cute little half-smile.

"I'm guessing Alabama."

"You're close. Just right next door. Georgia." Her eyes fluttered on the name of her beloved state.

"So what brings you to Virginia?"

"Change of scenery."

"Well I hope you like what you see."

"So far, I do," she said looking me up and down. "I'll see you later, Honey, gotta catch my bus."

The next day, I met up with her at lunchtime in the school cafeteria. She told me that her family had moved from Georgia where her father had been a professor at a small college in some town I'd never heard of. "Just a frog's hop down the road from Savannah," she added when I shrugged ignorance. "Daddy taught biology there."

At first, Desiree didn't tell me the real reason for her family's move, but later I learned that her father had gotten into some kind of tiff with the college where he taught biology. "What was he doing, teaching evolution?" I asked her. I had heard my mom say that science teachers had to go light on that subject in some places, especially in the deep south.

"No, it was whales." Desiree said the word "whales" like they kept one as a pet. "It got into the newspapers that Daddy went out on a boat to try and stop some men from killing those poor whales. Did you know that over fifty thousand whales get killed each year? Isn't that the biggest crime you've ever heard off?"

"I had no idea."

"Well Daddy was trying to make a point so people would know what was happening. When he got arrested, the newspaper made it look like *he* was a criminal. And the school said, in so many words, that he was an embarrassment to them. So Daddy got a job up here teaching biology. We really like it here, you know."

It didn't take long before some other guys were trying to move in on Desiree territory. One of them was getting more of her attention than the others. He was a new kid at school, too, and I guess they felt a newcomer's kinship. Martin was his name. She told me Martin understood how hard it is to be accepted when you transfer to a new school where the cliques are up and running.

"No welcoming committee here," Desiree said, looking up and down the hallway. "Why, I told Martin that girls are much worse than boys about accepting somebody new. And I think he agreed with me."

"Just tell them you transferred here from reform school."

"You've got to be kidding."

"That's what I'd do."

"Why you're just something else."

When Desiree walked down the hallway, the female hall veterans who huddled together every morning chattering away like a bunch of clucking chickens would go silent. The faces of the five or six girls in each huddle would turn to follow Desiree. Once she was down the hallway they'd turn back to face each other and their clucking would start all over again with quick glances in the direction of her departure.

"It's like in those cowboy movies when the wagon trains get in a circle to fight off the Indians," I told Desiree.

"I guess they think I'm just going to scalp them." Desiree gave a little wave of her hand, dismissing it all. "The silly things. Now what would I want to do with *their* hair?"

Desiree's parents seemed friendly and tried to fit into their new neighborhood. On weekends her father would be out in the front yard throwing the football with Desiree's little brother, Jonah, (of course—the whales) and he would give a big wave to everyone who drove by. Desiree's mom greeted me like I'd just brought them a bag of freshly ground grits. When I had a date with Desiree, Mrs. Duncan would invite me into her kitchen for lemonade or ice tea. While I waited for Desiree to finish dressing, her mom would chatter away with her sweet Georgia accent telling me how much they loved living in Virginia.

"I just can't get over how cool the nights are here," she told me. "Where we come from, September is just as hot and muggy as August and the bugs just eat you alive. I know you must love it up here."

"Yes Ma'am. Not too many bugs."

"You know, I'm really looking forward to trying some of your Virginia country ham."

"You should. It's real good."

"They tell me it just melts in your mouth."

"Yes Ma'am, it does." I always thought it was too salty but I didn't want to say anything to spoil it for her.

"I do believe your crickets are louder than ours."

"They'll get louder right before frost. Like they're singing a goodbye song."

"Whew. If they get much louder we're gonna have to stuff our ears with cotton when we go to bed at night." Mrs. Duncan tapped her ears, and then smiled to let me know she was just kidding. She also wanted to know about the school, if I liked my teachers and did I make good grades. She asked about my father's work and the church I went to. Of course she wanted to get a feeling for this new kid her daughter was dating. But they only let me take Desiree out on dates one night each weekend. It was either Friday night or Saturday night. But not both. They didn't want her to go out with the same guy all the time, nothing steady. Now I can see the danger in that, but back then it created a bit of trouble for me.

That trouble was mainly because of one other guy,

Dickie Basham, who didn't even go to our school. I think Desiree met him at her church and he latched onto her like a tick on a dog. I knew him from the Boy Scouts and before that, from elementary school. That was when we lived in the old part of town, near the river. Basham was a real prick. I don't often call people names but I'll call him one any day. It was one of life's cruel jokes that this guy ever showed up again in my life after my family moved to the county district and I changed schools. Basham and I had been patrol boys at the same elementary school. Wearing our white patrol belts and badges, we would be on little-cop duty holding our arms out to keep other kids from crossing the street until it was safely free of traffic. We were even allowed to stop traffic. I was really proud I had been selected to be a patrol boy. It was an honor and it got us out of class early to station ourselves at the crosswalks. One day Basham told the principal he saw me climbing a tree rather than doing my patrol duty at the crosswalk.

"Mrs. Vulmer, I saw him hanging out of the tree when he should have been on duty," Basham stated, giving me a dismissive glance.

Why he volunteered that I'll never know. It was a total lie, but because he was older than me, and captain of the patrol boys, the principal believed him and gave me a real tongue lashing about being irresponsible. Basham's accusation had left me speechless. I just couldn't figure it. I thought I was going to lose my badge and belt. Mrs. Vulmer told me I could keep my job if I promised I would take my duty seriously in the future.

After thinking about her offer, I took off my belt and badge and handed them to her. That was probably just what Basham wanted me to do. "He's a damn liar and you can get somebody else to stand out there in the rain," I told her. Mrs. Vulmer, of course, called my parents to tell them I had used profanity in her presence.

Also, Basham had been the leader of my Scout group, the Iroquois. He was one of the reasons I quit the Scouts. He loved the marching and saluting and all that military stuff and he outranked me there as well. He had earned Star ranking while I was still First Class. Being in uniform, standing in attention during parade drills, that was his thing rather than camping out and hiking

Desiree invited me in one day when I stopped by and there was Basham sitting at her dining room table with his elbows on a scrabble board. It was the same smug guy, only not in his Boy Scout's uniform. I couldn't believe it. I half expected him to pull out some of his merit badges and wave them in my face.

"We're engaged in a very intellectual game," he said looking up from the scrabble board as though even shooting marbles would be a challenge for me.

He had a smirky pretty-boy face and took pride in the quirkiest stuff. "We're the only family anywhere around here that regularly uses blackstrap molasses," he'd told me once as though that was supposed to impress me.

"So what?" I asked him.

"There's a lot of iron in molasses that helps you transport oxygen."

"So?"

"So you need oxygen for your brain to work better. But you wouldn't know about that." Basham squeezed a satisfied little smile at me.

"So why not go lick the railroad track?"

"Railroad tracks are made from steel. There's a big difference between iron and steel. That's why."

"Well now, how about that."

"Steel contains carbon which makes it stronger than iron."

"Oh yeah, carbon. Glad you straightened me out on that. I could have gone through life thinking iron was it.

Amazing what a little carbon can do."

"It's the basis of life on our planet," he had to add.

"What about water?"

Having to share Desiree with that bastard got to me. It wasn't jealousy or my picturing him going further with her than I did. No, she wasn't going to let anybody get a hand on her panties. Not just yet. Desiree let it be known she was saving herself for her husband to be. She told me Basham wasn't really into physical contact anyhow. Pure love was his thing, he told her. Maybe she wanted me to feel secure about our relationship—like she was saving her best kisses for me. I suppose I should have been relieved but somehow I wasn't. Bashing Basham's nose was the only physical contact I could imagine with him.

If his love was pure, mine was applied. As soon as I opened the car door for her and watched her slip onto the seat with her skirt riding half way up her thigh, I started thinking about safe places to go park. And she always smelled delicious—like freshly sliced white peaches on a humid summer night, and I was one hungry boy.

"Can you feel my heart beating?" she said to me one night when we were sitting in my car, fogging the windows while rain splattered down on the car roof. "It's beating in time to the raindrops."

I checked her heartbeat. "Wow. Pretty amazing. A lot stronger right here," I said, taking full advantage of the opportunity to slip my hand under her bra.

"Of course. And it beats even faster when you do that."

I didn't bother to check my own heart but I'm sure it was pounding faster than a drum roll for kickoff. When I put my hand on her leg, she lifted it back to her heart and held it there.

"This is where love resides, Honey," she said, holding my hand over her pounding heart.

I don't know if Basham was into heartbeats or what he did with her. She said Basham told her they were intellectually compatible which is why he liked her. Maybe they did crossword puzzles when they went out or took the scrabble board. I don't know. Or maybe they discussed carbon bonding. Or iron ore smelting. I hope she didn't call him "Honey" the way she said it to me. She could say honey like it was dripping off the spoon and right into her mouth.

She told me Basham didn't drink. And she didn't either. "I just know how terrible liquor is for everybody," she announced so often it made me sometimes miss other girls I knew who would drink beer and sip a little bootleg or bourbon whenever I could get hold of it. But not Desiree. Around Desiree you'd have thought alcohol was the devil's fruit juice. I pictured Basham reaching under his car seat and pulling out his black strap molasses and offering her a swig. He'd even have it wrapped up in a brown paper bag.

Sometimes Desiree dated the new kid, Martin. If I had my choice, I'd rather see my almost-girlfriend go out with him than Basham. She said Martin was a nice guy whose favorite thing to do was go to a drive-in restaurant for a milkshake. Seemed to me like a good thing for them to do. She said he liked movies, too, but he wasn't a good dancer and she loved to dance. Since he wouldn't take her dancing, I had him beat on that one. Another friend's mother, Miz Bonny Gilwall, taught me to dance and we practiced almost every time I went over to her house (that comes later). I knew Basham couldn't dance. He moved like his shoelaces were tied together.

Martin went out for football, and Desiree took in some of the games when he played on Friday nights. He was big (thanks probably to all those milkshakes) and played tackle, but Martin wasn't on the starting team (maybe too many milkshakes).

I had played on the team the previous year but I didn't get through the season. I didn't get injured. Football just interfered with my other passion—horses. Sometimes I worked at Mr. Hamlyn's equestrian center on weekends or rode at another stable, Charlie Arnaberry's. And then I had horseshows to take in. Football games were usually on Friday night. Sometimes they were on Saturdays. That's when I had a problem. One weekend, Mr. Hamlyn called and asked me if I could help him out at a horseshow that some of his riders were participating in. It was a big show and they needed extra hands with horses. It was the last horseshow of the season. It just so happened that our football game fell on a Saturday that weekend. Huge conflict for me. I thought it might be tricky trying to explain to the coach that I was going to have to miss the game that weekend because of a horse show. And it was.

"It's your choice—football or horses," he snapped.

"It's a chance for me to make a little extra money," I offered, thinking the word money might carry some weight.

"Football is a team sport and you don't abandon your teammates in mid-season."

He didn't ride horses, so I'm sure he didn't understand my feelings. I mean, to him football was everything. Especially winning.

"Okay, I'll clean out my locker right now," I told him. I think he was surprised, but he didn't know I loved horses almost more than girls and a heck of lot more than football.

I'd given him more information than I needed to. Maybe I was too honest. I could have crossed my fingers and told him my appendix was flaring up and my doctor said no contact sports or the little thing would rupture for sure. I hate to say it, but school taught me that lying rather than honesty is the best policy. At least in some situations. Being a freethinker, I finally put it all together: be honest with individuals but schools are institutions and you tell institutions whatever fits their rules. Consider the situation and who and what you're dealing with. Then get creative or they will screw you over big time.

I don't think Martin got into many games, but he did score some points with Desiree by being a player on the team. Of course, football practice every afternoon kept him pretty busy, but they managed to find some time for dating. Suiting up for a game in the football team uniform helped Martin get accepted by the guys at Jubal Anderson, and going out with him allowed Desiree a chance to convince some of the girls on the ad hoc social acceptance committee that she wasn't a threat to them. She had narrowed her school choice of guys down to Martin and me. No loss to any of them.

I did take Desiree to the big Christmas dance at school. We went in a car I bought with money I'd made working at the stable -- a 1949 Pontiac Silver Streak. Got it for $195. The car needed a lot of work, so I hadn't driven it much. A week before the dance I got busy working on the car. My dad helped me put some new plugs and points in it. Then we did some touch-up painting. By the evening of the dance I had a real machine. I thought it would really impress Desiree to go in my own car rather than my mom's DeSoto. And it did. She made a big deal over the car when she saw it.

"That's the car you've been telling me about?"

"Yep. Not much, but she's all mine."

"Not much? Piffle. Why Honey, this car's a classic. How on earth did you ever manage to talk someone into parting with a treasure like this?"

I held the door for her and when she slipped onto the seat she slid over to the middle so she could be right up against me.

At the dance, we put on such a performance that one of the teachers roped into chaperone duty for the night called us Fred and Ginger. Desiree was seasonally dressed in a spruce green dress with a white silk scarf at her neck, a red ribbon in her hair and shoes she had painted gold. I thought she looked gorgeous. Whether it was slow dancing or rocking around the clock, we had all the right moves.

Martin was there with some girl named Brenda. Martin's eyes were on Desiree every time I looked to see if he had gotten beyond clutching his date and swaying his head and shoulders back and forth. Only two other guys broke in to dance with Desiree and they soon realized they weren't in the same league with me. Oh, but they were envious. I could tell by the way they were talking to each other while looking at us on the dance floor. I'd learn there was a price to pay for showing off with your dance date.

When we went out to get into my car that I'd left in the one unlighted spot in the school parking lot—thinking it would be a good dark place for some after dance smooching—somebody had slashed a couple of my tires. I don't know when I ever felt so sick. But then I was glad they hadn't put a knife in the tires on my mom's car. If it had been one tire, I had a spare and could have solved the problem, but two flat tires at midnight is a major situation.

Even though it was midnight, Desiree called her folks to tell them I had a car problem and we'd be late. Her father offered to come pick us up but she told him I had already called for a taxi. Desiree must have felt sorry for me because, in the back seat of the taxi, she kissed me like we were playing a movie role and I was heading off to war the next day. She even let me put my hand on her legs. Maybe she was in the Christmas spirit of giving. We both got out of the taxi at her house. It was the only house on the block with Christmas lights still on at that hour, a few white lights her father had strung around the front door. I had just enough cash to pay the driver. The walk from Desiree's back to my house wasn't too far—about a mile. Since the dance wasn't over until midnight and we didn't get back to her house until nearly 1:00, her parents had gone to bed knowing their daughter was safely on the way home. Usually she had to be home by eleven, but they had made an exception for the Christmas dance.

Desiree took off her gold shoes and tiptoed back to her parents' bedroom and peeked in on them. When she came back to the living room, she motioned for me to take off my shoes and bring them along. Then we tiptoed back to her bedroom, went in and she locked the door. Their house was, fortunately, all on one floor and her parents' bedroom was at the far end of the hallway with Jonah's bedroom next to hers. She stepped over to her bedroom window and raised the sash.

"That's how you're leaving," she whispered. "Any problems with that?"

I looked out the window, checked the distance to terra firma and formed my exit plan. I could see it wasn't much of a drop to the ground and only a couple of small shrubs to avoid. "No problem," I assured her and lowered the window sash.

"Where are the screens?" I asked in a whisper.

"Put away for the winter." She said it so softly I could barely understand her.

Desiree untied my tie and tucked it into my jacket pocket. Then she pulled my jacket off and placed it carefully over the arm of a chair. She turned off the light switch, pulled the ribbon from her hair and started undressing right in front of me. The only light in the room spilled in through the window from the Christmas lights strung around the front door. Not much, but probably just enough for her comfort. First the scarf, then the dress came off. She stood there for a moment in her white slip just staring at me before pulling it over her head. Then off came the bra and panties. The performance was her Christmas present to me and I couldn't have asked for anything nicer, although more lighting would have been a blessing. She must have known my thoughts for she stepped over by the window where the light was better, or maybe my eyes had adjusted to the dark. I held up my hands motioning for her to stay right where she was so that I could admire her porcelain skin and that dark triangle at the top of her legs. I waved my hand in a circle and she did a slow pirouette lifting her arms over her head like a ballet dancer. I started unbuttoning my pants but she rushed to me putting her hands on mine. "Don't take them off. You've got to be ready to run, Honey," she purred. Taking my hand she led me over to her bed. She lifted the covers and crawled under them, then held the covers up for me to slip into the bed beside her. She was shivering so I held her tightly and kissed her until we both were putting out enough heat to glow like a Christmas ornament. Eventually she fell asleep in my arms. How she could snooze off under conditions like that is beyond me. There was no way I was going to get any sleep. But I enjoyed every minute of being in bed with her and touching her wherever I wanted.

When I heard the toilet flush somewhere down the hallway, I got up, slipped on my shoes and jacket, grabbed my overcoat and opened the window. That time it creaked. It hadn't made any noise before. Desiree sat up in bed, putting her finger to her lips. "Sshhhh."

I tossed my overcoat onto the lawn and climbed out the window, feet first, one leg then the other and ducked my head through, then pushed myself away and landed with a thump that might have gotten her folks' attention in warm weather when their windows were open. But it was blessedly cold outside. When I reached back to close the window, Desiree leaned out and whispered, "Merry Christmas." I stood on my tiptoes and we kissed once more. Then she carefully closed the window while blowing me kisses.

When I picked up my overcoat, there were snowflakes on it! I looked up at the sky, which had filled with snowflakes drifting lazily to the ground. It seemed funny how the white flakes of snow looked dark against the sky. I guess it's because you see the shadow side when you look up into the sky, even at night. I felt like lying down in Desiree's yard and letting the snowflakes melt on my face, which was in need of cooling off. But I thought I'd better get going in case her parents or little brother happened to look out one of the windows at the body lying in the yard and call the police. I shook the snow off my overcoat, pulled it on and headed for home.

The first few hundred yards were easy going because the snow was melting as soon as it touched the road, but it was already sticking in the grass beside the road and on the shrubs and trees in the yards along the way and even the rooftops were turning white. Soon the snow was coming down hard enough to cover the road, and the footing was getting slick. I could take a few running steps, and then skate and slide along the road. The way the snow was beginning to fall and swirl made me feel like I was in one of those snow globes you turn upside down. The only sounds were the muffled scraping and squeaking of my feet in the snow and my breathing. When snow falls like that, all the sounds stay close, making the world your very own. There were a few Christmas lights, decorations, glowing on some of the houses along the road I lived on; the red colored lights stood out even brighter against through the falling snow. But inside the houses were all dark. And that magical world was all mine.

One car finally passed by, clunking tire chains already. I didn't even think about trying to hitch a ride. In the car's headlights the snow looked like a blizzard. And by then it might have been. By the time I got to my house my footsteps were crunching and my feet freezing. Once inside, I could see it was almost 4:00 a.m. And not a creature was stirring in the house, not even a mouse, as far as I could tell.

The snow turned out to be the biggest snowfall on record for December. When I looked out my bedroom window the next morning, I saw the snow still falling like white sheets shaken out from the heavens. Halfway home from Desiree's house, I had begun to wonder about practical matters like did she get up and brush her teeth, put on a nightgown, and pee and did I leave identifiable footprints beside her bedroom window when I jumped out? Seeing the amount of snow already on the ground gave me a warm secure feeling that nobody was going to notice those footprints any time soon. I went back to bed dreaming of Desiree.

My mom poked her head into the room a couple of times to see if I was still breathing. Once, when she saw I was awake, she asked me about my car.

"Somebody slashed a couple of tires," I told her.

"That's terrible. Did you call the police?"

"The police? Why would I call the police?"

"Slashing tires is a crime," she snapped.

"What are the police going to do, get finger prints?"

"They could file a report."

"Why didn't I think about that?"

Mom closed the door quietly and left me alone.

Considering the snowfall, there wasn't any chance I was going to see my car any time soon, so I slept most of the day. Anyhow, it was Sunday and I didn't have much to do except work on a book assignment. Our English teacher, Mrs. Wattles, had assigned *Jane Eyre* for the holidays. Every guy in the class had groaned. She could have given us a choice of books but she said it was one of her favorites and, since it was a classic, we should know it. After we read the book we were supposed to write a paper on greed and connect it to the story. Reading about that girl's trapped life wasn't easy when I was cooped up at home. I read a little and went back to sleep. I got up just before dark and checked on the snow. Deep. Over a foot and still coming down in a fury.

I called Desiree and thanked her for going with me to the dance. "And everything else," I added without being specific. She told me that she and her mother were baking cookies to take to friends. "I hope they're in easy walking distance."

"Does it always snow here like this?' she asked.

"No, this is something special I did just for you."

"Wow. I've never seen anything like this. I mean, in Georgia we might get a heavy frost, but when I look out the window I keep expecting to see reindeer prancing through the yard. It's just something else. I can't tell you how excited I am."

"Wanted to get you in the Christmas spirit," I said.

"You sure did, Honey."

After I hung up the phone, I turned on the floodlights, put on some slow jazzy music and watched the snow show. Falling snow is beautiful to watch, but when it starts piling up it does make problems for someone as restless as I am. I mean like how long could I stay cooped up in the house with family? But I wasn't going to think about that just then. I wanted to think about Desiree and watch the snowflakes fall.

The next morning I got a phone call from Mr. Hamlyn at the stable. He wanted to know if there was any way I could get out to his farm and help him clean some stalls and exercise some of the horses. He said Moggins had gone to visit his wife's family in Richmond and couldn't get back because of the snow. Lewis couldn't get out nor could Curtis.

Riding-school horses stay fit because they are used to regular work but with a snow this deep they were going to be standing in their stalls getting rank. Mr. Hamlyn couldn't just turn them out because they'd hang around the gate pawing the snow and kicking at each other.

"You can count on me," I told him although I didn't have any idea how hard it would be to hike in snow that deep. The equestrian center wasn't that far from my house and there were shortcuts through the woods. With nearly two feet of snow, snowshoes would have been the way to go, but who had snowshoes in Virginia?

Mr. Hamlyn's call was my salvation. I could get out of the house and get moving. I decided to pack some things in a knapsack in case I couldn't get back and needed to stay over at his farm. I could relate to those horses standing up in their stalls. I had only been shut in for a day and I had spent most of that time sleeping, but I was rearing to go. I put my riding boots and a change of clothes in my knapsack. The snow looked deeper than the height of my galoshes so I put on my some canvas hunting pants my father got for me. I had never used them. I tied the cuffs over the galoshes.

"You have your gloves?" my mom asked me as I was heading out the door.

"Two pair."

"And what about your galoshes?"

"Of course." I showed her how I had tied the pants over them.

"I hope that works."

"Don't worry. It will."

"Call me and let me know you got there safely."

"Yes, Ma'am."

The snow had settled into a few flurries and the sky was still grey but the air was as crisp and clean as it can ever be. All during my hike over to the farm I thought of Desiree. I relived the scene of her coming out of her clothes and longed for a repeat performance. But that was not to be.

When I finally got to the stable, I found Mr. Hamlyn in one of the stalls rubbing bacon grease into the horse's hooves. We did it to all the horses we planned to ride. It was a wet snow and the bacon grease would keep the snow from balling up inside their hooves.

We opened the barn doors and mounted up inside the stable. The snow was so deep that our horses just stopped and looked at it when they got to the doorway. They snorted and stomped like we'd played some big trick on them. After the horses got a good look at the snow, Mr. Hamlyn put his heels to his horse, and Rubber Ball lived up to his name, leaping off all four feet out into the snow, landing in it up to his knees. My horse, Holligan, showed more caution and curiosity. He stepped out in the snow, dropped his nose down to it, snorted and starting pawing.

We headed off toward the back hay field letting the horses pick their way until they got a feel for the footing. They pranced and jigged with ears up, necks arched, tense as coiled springs. We tried to keep them at a walk until we got out to the hay field that was open and flat, a good place to let them off the bit. As soon as we did, they took off plunging through the snow trying to canter. The snow was so deep that the horses had to leap and dive through it. Full of themselves, they tried to buck, and if my horse had gotten his head down low enough he might have thrown me. Leaping and plunging, we went across the field in the knee-deep snow. The horses kicked up clumps of snow over our heads and Mr. Hamlyn roared with laughter. We both did.

We rode all afternoon, exercising two horses at a time until we had taken the edge off all sixteen of the schooling horses. I laughed at the energy and antics of some of these normally placid schooling horses having a playful romp in the snow.

I stayed over at Mr. Hamlyn's house that night. I didn't have the energy to hike home, and he wanted me to stay and help him until Moggins got back. And I wanted to stay. I called Mom to let her know. She wanted to make sure I was warm and she asked if I had dry clothes. She told me she had heard about people getting frostbite.

Mr. Hamlyn didn't have much to eat except for some venison and boiled potatoes and a fruit cake one of the rider's mothers had brought him. He took a few shots of Kentucky bourbon along with his dinner and left the bottle on the table for me.

"I am not going to serve you alcohol, but if you want to serve yourself, I never saw you." He laughed as he put another shot glass in the middle of the table.

I helped myself—two shots to wash down the deer meat, another for the fruitcake and another for good luck. After that I could hardly drag myself from the table.

We got up early the next morning and headed for the stable to clean stalls. Later we rode, getting his boarding horses exercised. It was another perfect day for snow riding. Late in the afternoon, the sun finally broke through the clouds. Road crews were beginning to make some headway clearing the main roads. We put chains on Mr. Hamlyn's car so he could drive to the train station downtown to pick up his wife who was coming home from one of her many trips to New York. He dropped me off at my house on the way. I needed to get home for Christmas, too, even though I would have just as soon stayed over at his farm and kept riding.

When I got home, my mom told me some girl had called but she didn't leave a message. I tried to call Desiree but there was no answer. I kept calling but never got an answer. I guessed that they had gone to visit her family for the holidays once the roads were passable.

Nearly two feet of snow and not being able to get to my car did put a crimp in my lifestyle. On the positive side, I managed to get the paper on greed in *Jane Eyre* written. I even had enough time left to proofread it. I felt pretty good about that. I cleaned it up enough to get a B+ on the paper, the highest grade Mrs. Wattles ever gave a male student as far as I know.

It took nearly a week before the snow was cleared from the school parking lot and I could start digging my car out. Then I had to haul my tires to a garage in the trunk of a friend's car. One tire was patchable but the other one wasn't, so I had to buy a retread from the garage. By the time I got my old Pontiac Silver Streak rolling again it was the day before school was due to be back in session.

During the Christmas holidays I kept calling Desiree's house, but there was no answer. Driving by her house, I didn't see their car in the driveway. And the Christmas decorations around the front door stayed dark. When school started again after the New Year, I took the school bus and looked for Desiree on it but she wasn't there. Everybody on the bus was chattering away about their Christmas gifts and all the problems the snow had created for them.

It wasn't until second period at school that I got the news about Desiree. I should have known something was up by the way several of the girls in the hallway were looking at me—that look of pity mixed with curiosity about how I was handling whatever was going on. I had begun to worry that something really bad might have happened to Desiree's family, like getting stuck in a snow bank and freezing to death. Her father wasn't used to driving in snow. My imagination was racing. There had been no car in their driveway. No answer on their telephone. I had not had a word with her since the phone call the second night of the snowstorm. But the truth was staggering: Desiree had gotten married over the holidays! And she was pregnant!

Once it hit, rumors raced around the school faster than germs in a crowd of sneezing kids. Surprisingly, it was her other boyfriend, Martin, who gave me the news, the real scoop. He had called to wish her a Merry Christmas and she told him she was moving back to Georgia.

"Your whole family up and leaving?" he had asked her. "No. Just me. I'm going to have a baby and I'm going back to Georgia to be with the baby's daddy." Martin repeated her words over and over like he was rehearsing lines for some stage play and not sure he was getting them right. And his words seemed as unreal to me as if they had come out of a school theatrical production. Martin told me her family had gone to South Carolina with her for a civil wedding of some kind, he said. Apparently, she and her old boyfriend had had an emotional goodbye before her family moved north from Georgia. And they had gotten carried away.

"Married! You're kidding!" I finally managed.

"I wish."

"And a baby! She's going to have a baby!"

"That's what she told me."

"In South Carolina?"

"No. The family went there for a quickie wedding. Then back to Georgia to get her settled in. Help her and her boyfriend ... I mean, husband, find an apartment."

Martin looked like he could use a milkshake. I thought he was about to lose it after he told me everything he knew. It was sad seeing a big guy like that with tears in his eyes. I put my arm around his shoulder and tried to console him. I guess he was really smitten by her. I mean, I was, too, but I must have been in a state of shock and somehow comforting Martin left me detached from the reality of it all. At least for a while.

"Teddy," I finally announced, putting it all together.

"Teddy what?"

"She told me she had a boyfriend back in Georgia and that he wrote to her every week. Teddy is what she called him. He played baseball for their school. A pitcher. He wanted to pitch in the big leagues some day. He had been her teddy bear," she said. Something in me wanted to add, "She and her Teddy must have gotten bare at some point." But I let it go. Martin might not see the humor in it. The bell rang and Martin wandered off down the hallway, his big shoulders drooping like he'd lost all his stuffing.

I was late for biology class, and Mrs. Darlrimple glared at me as I slid into my seat. If she had heard the gossip, couldn't she have shown a little understanding? Of course not. She even drove the spike in deeper, lecturing us on asexual reproduction in fungi. As though that was the answer. No little gametes getting together. I didn't need any more reminders. And I bet Mrs. Darlrimple would never go to bat for whales like Desiree's father had done.

With Mrs. Darlrimple chattering away and drawing fungi spores on the blackboard, I spaced out and started reliving the night in bed with Desiree. My God, she was with child and there we were so close to ... doing it, and my hand roaming over her tummy never expecting that beneath her soft smooth skin was a newly beating little heart. And I thought I was good at feeling heartbeats. Amazing, all that time she was carrying some guy's child! I wonder when she found out?

Her parents had been right—but a little late—setting

the rules on not dating just one boy. But on the bright side, she had saved herself for her husband. And she got to move back to Georgia. Desiree had done a good job of passing herself off as a virgin for a few months. She sure looked as pure as my grandmother's China doll. So that was a plus. Those girls in the school hallway honing their judicial skills had probably been on the mark about her all along. And they had to feel good about sensing who had an intact hymen and who didn't. And I wouldn't have to see Basham or even hear about him anymore. Then, too, I had learned how to share something precious—Desiree—an important lesson for maintaining sanity. So in the balance, it wasn't a total disaster after all.

After school was out I didn't want to go home so I headed over to Mr. Hamlyn's stable. He wasn't there. Nobody was there but Moggins who was crimping oats, getting ready to feed the horses.

"What the hell's wrong with you?" he asked when he turned the crimper off.

"Nothing."

"Did they throw you out of school?"

"No."

"Girlfriend dump you?"

"Something like that."

"You want a drink?" Moggins nodded toward the sacks of oats where he kept his bottle.

"Sure." Moggins reached under a bag of oats and pulled out a pint of something with a buffalo on the label. I took a couple of swallows. It burned all the way to my knees. At least that's what it seemed like. I walked over to a stall and looked in at Marigold and told her how much I loved her. She glanced at me and went back to munching hay.

When I got home I could smell pork chops frying. Only bacon can make a kitchen smell better. But I wasn't hungry. I told Mom I had a paper to write. "Hold my pork chops," I told her. "If I don't get this in by tomorrow I'm gonna fail history." She just shook her head.

I went to my room, locked the door and tried to write something about Desiree but I just stared at the blank page. She had kept so much from me and had not even told me goodbye. She didn't even send me a farewell note. Maybe she tried to call me when I was staying over at Mr. Hamlyn's farm. It might not have been her who called. I think it was. I think, too, she had begun to like me—I mean, really like me—and under the circumstances she had given me all she could. And she knew it had to be a clear break. She knew, too, we'd always have that night of the Christmas dance, the night just before the big snowfall.

Midnight's Sidekick

After Desiree, I dated a few girls from the school but I was just going through the motions of dating. No other girl made me feel special the way Desiree had. I missed being called all those confectionary names and with a Georgia accent that made me feel like we were swinging in a hammock together on a balmy day while licking cake icing off each others' fingers. But Desiree didn't ride. She was actually scared of horses. I knew that once spring arrived and horseback riding season really got underway, I'd have to make a choice. And just like with football, horses would have won.

On Saturdays, I rode in the arena with some of the girls who came out to the stable, but I didn't go out at night with any of them. They had their own private school dances, their own Riggles Creek social life. They talked about some of the wild parties they had when their parents were away and they had somebody's house all to themselves. But they never invited outsiders. That was probably the only rule they had—no outsiders.

Beginning in the month of April, there was a horseshow every weekend somewhere nearby, and someone who boarded a horse at Mr. Hamlyn's or at Arnaberry's stable down the road always needed an extra hand getting a horse ready. So I could count on making a little extra money and having a good time at the show.

The Greater Southwest Virginia Celebration of the Horse was held early in the month of May. It was the show of shows, the first major show of the season, the one where trainers brought out their new horses. The Celebration of the Horse was a show for all breeds and riding styles, a weeklong show with hunters and jumpers, saddle horses, Morgans, Arabians, Tennessee Walking horses, and roadsters making up most of the entries. The show was held outdoors in a sort of natural bowl, a historically preserved site where there had been some major battle between the early settlers and the Indians they were trying to displace (and you know which side won). The place always made me feel a little weird, unsettled like some ghostly arrows were still flying through the air. But it was a beautiful piece of land. Maybe that's why they fought over it. Anyhow, I got in the Silver Streak and headed for the show, knowing somebody would need a horse cooled down.

Working at a horseshow doesn't involve a whole lot of labor. You get a horse groomed and saddled and ready for its class, then you watch it perform and walk it until the horse has cooled down. You put the horse in the stall and head back to the fence rail to watch the show. There's plenty of time to catch some of the classes. For me, the open jumping and the five gaited classes were the ones not to be missed. Those were the classes with the real equine athletes.

Sometimes, just for the hell of it, I liked to watch the

Tennessee Walking Horse classes because the walking horse people put on a spectacle beyond anything having to do with horses. These people are a subculture in the horse world; they enjoyed their own show circuit and seemed indifferent to the performance of any of the other breeds. It was said that jumping horses were for old money, saddle horses for new money, and walking horses for stolen money. Walking horse people owned used car dealerships or wrecking services or junkyards or discount furniture stores or stump grinding businesses. I don't know where they got their riding habits, but I hope they didn't spend much for them.

I'd heard there was going to be a real showdown on this particular night between a couple of good walking horses in the qualifying class, a roan mare owned by Preacher Rolle and a bay horse owned by a fellow named R. L. "Randy" Handy. The other eight or nine horses in the class would be also-rans (or also-walked in this case).

I had seen Preacher Rolle's mare show and remembered that she could move on at a running walk like she was heading for the stable at feeding time. Sure enough, on that night the mare hit the show ring at top speed, her ears up, head bobbing, and Preacher Rolle sitting smooth and tight in the saddle, grinning and singing, "I've got a ten dollar ring and I feel like a king on my Tennessee Walking Horse." Fortunately, Preacher Rolle's mare was a good-sized horse even for a Tennessee walker, because she had to carry a big man. Something about him reminded me of a mole, a giant mole sitting up there in the saddle. I guess it was his short arms with those wide hands and the way he rode, leaning forward with his shoulders pinched together, and that pointed no-neck face bobbing up and down like he was nibbling roots.

I never knew for sure whether or not he was a real preacher. Word was that he never missed a church service. Somebody told me that on Sunday mornings after loading up to leave the horse show grounds, he would head down the highway at the steering wheel of his horse van, keeping an eye out for a church. Any church, just so it had a steeple or something that looked like a steeple. At eleven o'clock sharp he'd be sitting in the pew commingling with the congregation regardless of the denomination of believers. "We all believe in the same God," he would tell people. "And even atheists reject the same God."

Like some singing cowboy out of those old western movies, he sang when he rode; only he wasn't singing about blue skies and doggies on the open range, he sang the walking horse song or he sang hymns. Leaning on the fence rail of the show ring, I caught what sounded like *Glory Be to Thee and Me* as he rode by.

Preacher Rolle owned a string of walking horses, but his roan mare, Roan Allen's Rebecca Rebel, was his best. The others were younger horses he was bringing along. He called the mare Becky Reb and everybody in the horseshow grandstands would start yelling Becky Reb, Becky Reb when they saw him heading for the show ring.

The only other real competition Becky Reb had was from a dark bay horse named Carbon Shaker's Big Man shown by R. L. "Randy" Handy. I got a kick out of watching him ride because he had long sideburns coming out from under a black fedora and he rode leaning back in the saddle with his feet stuck way out in front of himself like he was skidding to a stop. But that horse of his could move on with the best of them, head bobbing and hooves reaching out for new territory. Whenever I caught a walking horse class, it seemed that the Preacher and Randy Handy had the crowd's attention all to themselves. The two of them put on the show everybody came to see. Sometimes they would come down the straightaway at a running walk neck and neck with one trying to cover the other up, block the view of the show judge. But they did it in a kind of sporting way. You would have guessed that Handy and the Preacher were taking turns getting the blue ribbon.

Walking horses were the best trail horses nature ever came up with because they could move along at that gliding gait, do it all day and never seem to get tired.

I should explain right here that horses are born with either an inclination to trot (a diagonal gait) or pace (a lateral gait). Horses that have a lateral swing to their gait become amblers or walking horses or racing pacers. Five gaited American Saddle horses are a rarity in that they can be trained to go both ways—trot and do the ambling "slow gait" and rack (a smooth fast ambling gait with only one foot hitting the ground at a time).

Walking horses make it easy on the riders—none of the up and down posting to the trot. We always heard that the reason the Confederate cavalry regularly outperformed the Yankees, who had them outnumbered and better equiped, was that the rebs rode walkers or ambling horses that didn't wear the soldiers out getting to the battle doing all that posting for miles and miles. Robert E. Lee's horse, Traveler, was said to be a walker, but I don't know if that's true or not. The horse is stuffed and in the basement of some building at Washington and Lee University. I've seen him, and I didn't think he looked much like a walker now.

But turning this breed into show animals was a disaster. Some of the methods used to get the show horses to do their animated walk were just plain cruel like the "scoot juice"—a little bit of acid dripped on the horse's front feet to make them sore so they would pop their feet up high almost as soon as a foot hit the ground. When the Humane Society and the SPCA banned that, the walking horse people found other ways to get the same results, like tacks in the horse's front feet. The idea was to get them doing that "big lick" as they called it, a high stepping strut and doing it fast. They even tied false tails on the horses overtop of the real tail that was bent over a brace. A tail dragging the ground like a long skirt got you extra points with the judges, I guess.

A few walking horses, like Merry Go Boy or Midnight's Sun, could strut that high stepping running walk and do it naturally. Becky Reb was one of those horses and Carbon Shaker's Big Man was another. So it was that fight for first or second place in the show ring that got the crowd hollering. That was until thunder started rumbling that night.

The walking horse class was just getting underway and right before they closed the gate for the class, with Handy and the Preacher already getting their respective support crowds worked up and the Preacher wearing that self-satisfied grin, suddenly there was a really loud clap of thunder and the cheering stopped. All you could hear were these pounding hoof beats coming toward the show ring. Someone yelled out, "Clear the gate. Horse a-coming." At first I thought I heard more thunder, but it was hooves pounding the earth. Then a horse came out of the darkness and into the lights of the show ring and what a horse it was! Like a locomotive with steam blasting and whistles blowing, this big black horse with a yellow moon colored mane and tail roared into the show ring moving on like a racehorse, but it wasn't a racehorse and it wasn't running. The horse was doing this huge stretched out walk with his back feet outreaching his front feet, his head held high and proud, his neck arched, ears pricked forward and those front feet popping up so high he looked like he would hit himself in the chin. Up on his back was a little man with the face of a hawk, sitting straight up like he was at the dinner table, his brown Stetson pulled so low you wondered if he could see ahead of himself. His skin looked like it came from the same leather as the horse's saddle, dark and weathered. His eyes looked right into the crest of the horse's neck and he took no notice of the people in the grandstands.

Everyone stood up to get a better look at what was moving around the show ring. What they saw was a horse covering territory like a wildfire. Nostrils flaring, hooves flying, the horse's tail stretched out in the breeze behind him. Why, he was halfway around the track before the crowd could take in what they were seeing. And then they exploded, whooping and cheering wilder than if everybody there had just won the lottery and been guaranteed eternal salvation at the same time.

I was standing by the fence rail on the backside of the show ring, and I heard the man standing next to me say in a hushed voice, "That's Cade Pascal."

I'd never seen Cade Pascal show a horse. I'd heard his name and heard some of the stories about him, none of them good; but then horse people love to gossip, talk up the dirt on everybody. "What's the name of the horse?" I asked the guy standing beside me.

"Dunno," he said without turning away from that churning muscle and flying hooves kicking up dirt there in front of us. "But that's Cade Pascal alright."

One of the things I'd heard about Cade Pascal was that you had better lock up your wife and everything else you value when he's around. He had a reputation for being a womanizer and a thief. Good saddles had a way of disappearing when he was around. He never stayed in one place for very long, I heard. How could he with a reputation like that?

I never saw Cade Pascal give a signal to his horse but as the ringmaster signaled for different gaits (they do three of them) and the announcer called for them—"Now give me a flatfoot walk," that horse was strutting like he was leading the world's grandest parade. When the judge called for a running walk, all the horses in the show ring shifted into high gear and Pascal's horse started rambling on, passing them all, doing that 'big lick" as they call it and doing it right. Speed and motion—that's what the crowd came to see. When the announcer called for a canter, Cade Pascal pulled his horse back to a canter that made it look like he was in a rocking chair on a soft white cloud.

They reversed direction and started over again. When the show announcer called for a running walk Cade Pascal and his horse blazed by all the other horses like they were still coming out of the starting gate and he was moving down the backstretch. When the announcer called the horses in to line up, Cade Pascal didn't pay any attention until his horse had made another pass half way around the ring with the crowd going crazy. Finally he lined his horse up at the far end of the lineup and parked him out. When the judge walked up to inspect that horse, now all lathered with steam rising up off him like there was a fire in his belly, the crowd started whooping it up all over again. There was no way that judge could keep from giving the blue ribbon to Cade Pascal. There were ten places between his horse and the next one.

The judge turned in his card and took a seat under the judges' tent and the announcer called out, "The First Place ribbon goes to number 193, Midnight's Sidekick ridden by Cade Pascal." Once again the crowd went wild as Cade Pascal rode up to get his ribbon (and first place check). He took off his hat to the ribbon girl when she reached up to hand him his award. Then I could see those cheekbones and thick black hair that made you wonder if he wasn't some Indian Chief who accidently rode into the show ring. (I heard later he was part Cherokee.) Cade Pascal leaned over the horse's neck and hooked the blue ribbon onto the brow band of the bridle, and the photographer took his picture. Then

Cade Pascal rode up to the far end of the ring, away from the entry gate, to await the other riders getting second, third, fourth and fifth place ribbons.

After the last horse left the show ring, Cade Pascal turned Midnight's Sidekick loose for a victory pass—and I mean he turned the horse loose all the way around the show ring—with that blue ribbon waving like a flag in the wind. Then he did something I've never seen before or since. He dropped the reins on the horse's neck and with that horse churning up the track, Pascal reached into his breast pocket and pulled out a cigarette and a lighter. With his hands cupping his mouth to block the wind, he managed to light the cigarette. When he blew a puff of smoke into the air the crowd yelled even louder, if that was possible.

I was too far away to see what happened after that but someone told me later that as Midnight's Sidekick left the show ring one of Randy Handy's grooms yelled something at Cade Pascal who flipped his cigarette into the man's face and kept riding. Just about that time the storm broke with another clap of thunder and it started to rain.

I took off running up to the stable area after Cade Pascal and his horse. I had to have another look at that animal. No sooner had I found him than some man came running up out of the dark yelling, "Don't nobody do that to me and get away with it." Cade Pascal was just pulling the saddle off his horse, when he flipped the horse's reins over to me and started jumping around getting out of the way of this guy who was swinging a knife. They went running round and around the pickup truck and trailer with the man with the knife yelling and stabbing at the air. Cade Pascal finally got far enough ahead of him to vault over into the bed of his truck where he picked up a shovel and started swinging back at the man. Then Pascal jumped out of the truck bed and went after the man with them going the other way around the truck and trailer like they were unwinding. It was all happening so fast with the rain coming down hard like the sky was angry, and me trying to hold the horse and thinking I ought to get the saddle up off the ground before it gets soaked and muddy.

The fight quickly got a crowd of men gathered and Preacher Rolle was in the midst of them yelling, "Boys, boys cease your hostilities. Let the light and love of Jesus Christ shine upon you."

But it started raining harder and no light was shining as the man with the knife turned to run toward the stables and Cade Pascal caught him in the back of the head with the shovel and sent him sprawling into the mud.

Cade Pascal grabbed the horse's reins from me and led Midnight's Sidekick into the trailer. He never had a chance to walk the horse out and cool him down. He didn't even stop to pick up his saddle off the ground (maybe it belonged to someone else anyhow). He didn't even tie the horse up. He just pulled the bridle off, stepped out and closed the tailgate. He hopped into his pickup truck and rolled out of there. No headlights even, as that trailer bounced through the stabling area and out onto the highway. I guess he didn't want anyone to see what direction he was heading. Once he was down the road, he must have pulled over somewhere and taken the horse out and cooled him down. Even in the rain. I'd seen the steam rising off the back and neck of the horse while I was holding onto him. I would have been glad to cool him out. Just holding onto that horse made me feel like I'd touched something special.

I didn't mean to get caught up in it that night but I did. An ambulance came and picked up the injured man. The police came, too, and they asked me questions. I told them the truth. Some people said I'd been an accomplice but I wasn't. I never had a word with either man. All I did was hold the reins of the horse. When the man with the knife went after Cade Pascal, I was standing there beside his trailer, and Pascal tossed the horse's reins in my direction like I was a living hitching post. I caught the reins and held onto that big horse that stood watching the fight like he was enjoying seeing humans doing the action even if they were trying to kill one another.

A couple of nights later, I drove back over to the Greater Southwest Virginia Celebration of the Horse to see the championship classes. I was also hoping to find out what had happened after that fight. I saw the knife-swinging guy looking like somebody had painted deep purple pools under his eyes. Since the man hadn't been killed, I thought maybe there was a chance Cade Pascal and Midnight's Sidekick would be back for the championship class. I walked all over the stable area looking for Cade Pascal's Dodge pickup truck and his trailer. I couldn't forget what it looked like after what had happened that night. I looked in all the stalls that were set up for walking horses. I did see Preacher Rolle standing in front of a stall talking to one of his horses, or maybe he was singing a hymn to it. I didn't know Preacher Rolle except by sight, but I went right up to him and I said, "Excuse me Sir, but I was here a few nights ago and saw you show against a big black horse named Midnight's Sidekick and I was wondering if that horse is coming back here for the championship class?"

Preacher Rolle turned to me and said, "You saw that son? You saw that horse?"

"Yes Sir."

"Well, he won't be coming back. Thank the Lord."

"Nothing happened to him, did it? I mean I've never seen a horse like that before."

"He's gone back to hell, son."

"Cade Pascal's in hell?"

"No son, the horse. Didn't you know that horse was the devil incarnate?"

I didn't quite get what Preacher Rolle was saying. I just stood there until I managed, "What did you say?"

"The devil! The devil can take many forms, my boy."

"You're telling me that horse was the devil?"

"The very incarnation of sin. But I prayed that he never visit us again and my prayers have been answered."

"You're trying to tell me I was holding the reins of the devil?"

"Are you the lad that held Cade Pascal's horse while he took a shovel to poor Henry Skaggs?"

"Yes Sir. Pascal just flipped them to me after the man pulled a knife on him."

"Henry Skaggs wouldn't pull a knife on anyone unless it was self defense."

"Well he did. I saw him. But he'll think twice before he does something like that again."

"Son, I find this hard to believe."

And I found what he was saying hard to believe. Looking Preacher Rolle hard in the eye, I said, "I ran back here from the show ring to see Midnight's Sidekick up close. As soon as Cade Pascal got out of the saddle, that man came running up to him and he popped open a switchblade. Next thing I knew, I was holding the horse and Cade Pascal was dodging and ducking that knife until he jumped into the back of his truck and grabbed a shovel. I saw you come up. You got here just as Cade Pascal backed the guy up to the barn with the shovel. And I heard what you said. You tried to stop it."

Preacher Rolle drew a deep breath and clasped those wide hands together across his stomach and said. "He won't be back this way son. There's a warrant for his arrest. Whenever he shows up in the state of Virginia again, they'll nab him."

"But he did it in self defense."

"What—hit a man running from him? And after Pascal started it, flipping a cigarette in the man's face."

"I didn't see that part of it," I said.

"There's always more to a story than what you see on the surface. But the Lord sees it all."

"What about the horse?"

"He's back in hell, son. Back where he belongs. And you had a close call holding the reins of the devil. You could have been burnt!"

"I don't know about being burnt, but I've never seen a horse like that one."

"And you never will. Praise the Lord." Preacher Rolle turned and walked away from me swinging those short little arms like he was shaking off some dirt. Then he started humming. I think it was *Rejoice Ye Pure of Heart*, but I couldn't say for sure.

Even though I was now a freethinker, I couldn't help but wonder if Preacher Rolle was on to something because that big horse must have come from another world. Horses can't perform like that. Sometimes I think I dreamed the whole thing. And maybe I did. Even freethinkers can't control their dreams.

The Best Motel In Town

After holding onto the reins of the devil, some purification was definitely in order, even for a freethinker. And I'd soon get my chance.

Curtis Peddler, who had worked on and off at Mr. Hamlyn's called me one evening and asked if I could give him a ride over to the General Jackson Motor Lodge where he had taken a job as night manager. He told me his car was out of commission (not an uncommon occurrence) and he didn't want to take a taxi. I had gotten to enjoy Curtis because he had a bizarre sense of humor and he didn't mind putting rich kids in their place. Although we didn't hang out together, Curtis would show up from time to time with a six-pack of beer he needed some help with, and a lot of stories about the women and girls in our town, particularly the ones from Riggles Creek.

They had money to spend—those women who lived in the Riggles Creek section of town. They were the best looking, the best dressed, and drove the classiest cars and were obviously married to the men who kept the wheels of Weyridge commerce turning. Riggles Creek was the status area, our city's version of Hollywood, even if those tanned women weren't silver screen celebrities. So of course Riggles Creek garnered more gossip than any other section of town.

Riggles Creek Drive meandered for a half-mile or more through the most exclusive part of Weyridge, starting at the highway on the west border of the city and running all the way to the historic district downtown. The city fathers claimed they had been wise enough to leave a narrow stretch of undeveloped land along Riggles Creek as a community park and nature preserve (actually the land was in the flood plain so it couldn't be developed anyhow). On the hills across from the park were homes that had been built in the early days, back when the town still went by the Indian name of Waseka (meaning place of unusually large horseflies, according to Curtis.) Those early houses had been remodeled and maintained so that they had become stately. All the roads coming off Riggles Creek Drive led to newer homes bought by the up and coming professional class of lawyers, accountants, doctors, and managers of one business or another.

The General Jackson where Curtis worked was without a doubt the finest motel around. It was just off the far west end of Riggles Creek Drive on Highway 41 that skirted Weyridge. At one time it had been a show horse stable, but the owner had gotten tired of horses. He must have decided to make money instead of spending it and had done some major renovating. The grounds were almost as beautiful as they had been when mares and foals grazed in the pastures and some of the top show horses in the south were trained there.

On the way to the General, Curtis started ticking off the names of some of the Riggles Creek women who were making a little pin money "turning tricks," as Curtis called it, at the motel. Whether it was true or not, I was amused by Curtis' familiarity with the town's social register. But when one particular name popped out of his mouth—Pam Merkel—I exploded.

"There's no way in hell the Pam Merkel I know is turning tricks at the General or anywhere else!" I bellowed.

"Okay, okay—call it afternoon escorting," Curtis smirked. "They do it while their hubbies are at work." He realized he had gotten to me with this tidbit and was watching to see how far to push it. "I'm just telling it like it is."

"You're just making it up because you're so damn jealous of anybody from Riggles Creek."

"Right. Like I'd want to live around all those snobs."

"You damn right you would." I wanted to change the subject but Curtis had that look of a cop who had just spotted a parked car rocking on Lover's Lane. "They must not be paying you enough at the General."

He ignored my remark and kept on his track. "How do you know Mrs. Merkel?"

"She took some riding lessons at the stable. And she was always a lady. Mr. Hamlyn never got anywhere with her."

"She's a looker. Boy would I like to have a little of that."

"And she also taught Sunday school at my church when she and her husband first moved to town." Even bringing in the church didn't stop Curtis.

"Her husband's pulling in a lot of money managing Woodberries."

"How do you know that?"

"They live in Riggles Creek, don't they?"

"Then why would she be doing anything at The General if her husband's bringing in the dough? See—you just blew a hole in your story."

"Maybe her ole man's not doing enough for her. Too busy making money."

If anybody but Curtis Peddler had announced that bit of information about the afternoon-in-room escorting, I would have ignored it. But Curtis could collect dirt from an autoclave. He had a knack for finding out who was doing what to whom. He could have been a detective. Curtis was so engaging that people seemed to want to share all kinds of tales with him whether they were true or not. And he was always ready and willing to listen and learn.

Curtis had dropped out of school because he was bored and because the principal told him never to set foot in Jubal Anderson High School again. Everybody liked Curtis, even the teachers who were always having him expelled for some prank he pulled. They'd get flaming mad at him in class but you knew that deep down inside they got a big kick out of some of his antics. They probably couldn't wait to get home and tell their husbands what Curtis had done—like stealing the hubcaps off the police cars that were parked outside the school. He actually didn't steal the hubcaps, he just removed them temporarily in order to decorate the entrance to the school while the police were in the auditorium giving a presentation on driving safety.

When he left school for good, he got a job at Mr. Hamlyn's for a while. From there, he went on to a job waiting tables at the Rolling Hills Country Club where he managed to overhear conversations about everybody who was anybody. Curtis even had dirt on the manager of the club itself, Summers Johnston. "Johnston was manager of the Rolling Hills Country Club one day and not the next," Curtis told me. "Got caught in the sack with Dolman Morshanks' wife."

"Who is Morshanks?"

"Club president."

I didn't doubt Curtis on that one, nor did it surprise me because some of the girls I knew, whose families belonged to the club, told me about Summers Johnston. They said he got real touchy-feely with them around the club's swimming pool. He was a good-looking man and the girls liked chatting with him, although they knew that behind his sunglasses his eyes were peeling their bathing suits right off of them. "And he always offers to put suntan lotion on my back," one of the girls told me. "And that's not the only place he wants to put it," she added.

As for Mrs. Morshanks, she was apparently forgiven for her indiscretions by her husband, for both husband and wife continued to play golf together and dined at the club every weekend. Curtis told me that rich people don't get worked up about infidelity like middle class people do. "Money's what gets them worked up," he said. "Religion and all that moral stuff is a big deal only if you don't have money."

But Morshanks, Curtis said, still had to fire Summers Johnston for the sake of appearance, since some of the members of the club were clued in. Curtis waited on their table sometimes and he said Morshanks and his wife gabbed just like nothing had ever happened. "Never a cross word between them. Just goes to show you."

Not long after Summers Johnston took over the job managing the General Washington Motor Inn, Curtis followed him there. Or rather, knowing what a night-owl Curtis was, Johnston offered him a job. At the General, Curtis found a treasure trove of gossip since some of the locals used the motel for good-time get-togethers. "Best trysting place around," Curtis told me. He also told me that once Summers Johnston was established at the General Washington, some of the Riggles Creek women, who Johnston knew intimately, wanted to earn a little pin money. "They know Johnston can keep his mouth shut and match them with just the right class of salesmen passing through. They only do afternoon work, except for Doreen Von Hussman whose husband is in Richmond, serving in the General Assembly. She's the only one available for night jobs right now."

"Bullshit. You're just talking. Show me some proof. Bring me some pictures." I told Curtis he was just trying to sully the reputation of good people because no Riggles Creek girl would ever date him.

"At least those women picked the best motel around," Curtis said.

"You bastard!"

He had no real solid evidence that Pam Merkel was doing anything at the General Jackson Motor Inn. But he had definitely planted a seed. Maybe he was right about rich people not making a big deal over adultery. "Trailer park people shoot each other over sex all the time, but bigwigs try to act like they don't care," Curtis said. Sometimes he could announce scuttlebutt with all the authority of Edward R. Murrow giving out the evening news, so I couldn't help but wonder if he might have been on to something.

A few days later Curtis showed up at my house wearing a grin like he'd just talked his way out of a speeding ticket (which he was pretty good at doing). "You wanted proof. Here it is," he said, handing me a sheet of yellow notepaper.

I glanced over a list of names with phone numbers. "What is this suppose to be?"

"What do you think it is? It's the women doing ... well, I'll call it 'special hosting' or maybe *nude counseling* at the General since you don't like me calling it the hooker list."

"How in the hell did you get this?"

"I copied it from a list in Johnston's desk."

The fifth name down was P. Merkel. I just sat there totally stunned while Curtis grinned at me. He was so damned pleased at his detective work and I was so disheartened to see Mrs. Merkel's name, not to mention the names of several other women I knew of, including Dr. DuHon's wife. Dr. DuHon was an orthodontist who had made the news for being kicked out of the country club after being caught making it on a pool table with two of the female members (I guess the club had to set limits).

But Pam Merkel's name just blew me away. Then I thought—hold on; it just says P. Merkel. There could be other Merkels. Maybe Priscilla Merkel. Or Patty. I grabbed a phone book and looked up Merkel. Not a real common name and sure enough only one listed. And the phone number matched!

"But how do you know this is a hooker list?" I asked him. "It could be a list of women who do counseling. Or bake cookies for the guests. Or women he owes money to."

"Or maybe they owe money to him. He's got to get his pimp's cut."

"Curtis, you're making all this up. No woman from Riggles Creek is going to take a chance screwing some salesman passing through town. Besides, somebody would see their car."

"There's a closed garage where they leave their cars. It used to be the old hay barn out there. Remember? I've seen them park in it and sneak across the parking lot to the motel."

"I still don't believe you. Those women don't need any extra money."

"How do you know who needs money? Just because

they live around Riggles Creek doesn't mean their husbands give them all the money they need. And besides..." Curtis leaned into my face, "Maybe they do it because it feels good, because they need a little excitement, because living in Riggles Creek is so damn boring."

Curtis proved nothing to me except what a gossip and busybody he was. Still, I couldn't get Pam Merkel out of my mind. I kept picturing her at church wearing that wholesome smile of a missionary handing out free Bibles. I remembered her pointing to the maps of the Holy Land, locating the Hittites and Canaanites in time and place, telling us who they were and where they came from and where they went. And why. She had traveled to the Holy Land and I enjoyed hearing her talk about it, getting a firsthand account of what I could only image as desert with a lot of stucco buildings. Then I started thinking that she never taught any of the morality of the Bible, she stuck to history and geography. Maybe there was a reason she did that.

I remembered when she and her husband moved to town and joined our church. I thought she must have been a cheerleader when she was in college. She was so fresh and hopeful looking. I imagined her bouncing up and down on the sidelines during a football game, waving pom-poms and cheering on the team. Mrs. Merkel didn't seem like your typical Sunday school teacher. Actually, she wasn't much older than me, and the way she wore her hair in a cut that looked like Prince Valiant made her look even younger. But I never thought of her in a sexual way. That never crossed my mind.

My folks always discussed new people who joined the church. I could tell from my mother's tone which ones she approved of and which ones she didn't, although she never admitted disliking anyone. A foreign sounding name was always suspect. "Sounds German to me," she'd say and my father would nod like he understood what was wrong with that. The husband's line of employment was also important to my mom, but all I knew about Mr. Merkel was that he was transferred to town to manage Woodberrys Department Store.

"They've got a Yankee accent," my mom had said with a slight tone of concern. "They'll say things that are not said in good company." Being a southern lady, my mom was more comfortable with women who could add or stretch vowels when they greeted one another. ("It's soooo good to see you again.") When mom was introduced to Pam Merkel at church Mom said, "It's soooo nice to meet you." Pam Merkel shot back, "Likewise." Mom never got over that.

But I liked listening to Pam Merkel. Her words were sharp, clear, and distinct. Now the seed Curtis had planted in my mind wanted to grow and bear fruit, probably the deliciously juicy, tempting, and forbidden kind wearing bright red lipstick. I wanted the women in my life, the ones I admired, to be heroic; and heroes are not hypocrites. If Pam Merkel was turning tricks, she couldn't possibly still be going to our church. Such was my logic. So to put the matter to rest, the following Sunday I rolled out of bed, dressed in my Sunday best and went to church to satisfy my curiosity. I hadn't been there for several years but I had to see if Pam Merkel was still going. I mean, how could she go to church if Curtis was right? As a freethinker, I needed to form an opinion based on the facts. Then, too, it wouldn't hurt to get a little salvation going for me after holding onto the reins of the devil.

I drove downtown to the First Methodist Church of Weybridge—it was the third church built in Weybridge but the first for the followers of John Wesley. I parked the Silver Streak about a block from the church and walked, enjoying the bright sunlight, the crisp clean air and the feeling of righteousness churchgoers get on Sunday morning when they parade to their shrine.

Well, there she was standing alone just inside the narthex smiling at everyone and chatting the way church attendees do. She looked almost the same as she did the first day I saw her. The Prince Valiant haircut had grown down a little longer, but she still had the bangs and that cheerful fresh face. In a few moments her husband, who had been talking to two other men, joined her. She slipped her arm through his and the two of them walked down the center church aisle. She hadn't seen me come through the doorway. I watched her point to an empty pew and slip into it and then her husband settled in beside her. Since their pew was empty, I walked down the side aisle and slipped into the same pew and slid over beside her.

When she saw me, she gave me that pleased smile women get when they set something special on the dinner table. Pam Merkel patted my leg saying how good it was to see me back at church, then leaned all the way over to me giving me a whiff of her perfume while whispering, "I hadn't seen you here for awhile. I was hoping we hadn't lost you."

"Schoolwork, you know. Keeps me so busy," I whispered back, catching another whiff of her exotic scent.

"That's no excuse," she said with a tight-lipped smile, while giving her head a little shake as if she'd seen me taking too many cookies from the jar.

Obviously Curtis was wrong, and now I had to endure an hour of tedium for the price of my curiosity. Being a recently enrolled freethinker, it was going to be hard to sit through Reverend Swaim's sermon since it would be all about his opinions. I wanted to be back outside in the fresh air. Churches stay closed up too much of the time. They get stuffy and smell like a mix of cut flowers and hot candle wax in the bottom of a shoe closet. But sitting next to Pam Merkel and sniffing her perfume for an hour would get me through the ordeal.

Mr. Merkel was looking straight ahead at the minister, Reverend Swaim, who was installed on his throne behind the pulpit and appeared to be in reverent concentration. The stone face and tight set of Mr. Merkel's jaw left me wondering if he was anticipating being reminded of our sins or reflecting on the store inventory. Or was he harboring suspicions about his wife's activities? He seemed disconnected from her, totally absorbed in another world while she was very present and at ease in this one.

When the congregation was seated and settled, Reverend Swaim in his long black robe stood, stepped slowly to his lectern and began to turn the pages of a very large Bible until his fingers touched on the passage he wanted. "Proverbs," he said. And he read, *When He, the Lord, marked out the foundations of the earth I was here beside him like a master workman and I was his daily delight.* There was more but I don't recall it because I got stuck on the part about being His *daily delight* and all that could possibly mean. And was the speaker male or female? After reading the Biblical lesson, Reverend Swaim motioned for the congregation to rise.

Pam Merkel's stretched across me reaching for one of the hymnals that was in the rack on the back of the pew, sending up another cloud of her perfume. The angle of her reach allowed for a glimpse down her blouse—a red blouse with pearl buttons—that fell open revealing the lace of a white slip.

The congregation joyously sang "Blessed Be The Tie That Binds." After the hymn we remained standing to chant the Apostles' Creed. Then we took our seats in order to get to the substance of the day. When Pam Merkel reached across me again to replace the hymnal, I felt her breast press onto my leg. I wondered if she knew what she was doing. She could have handed me the hymnal to replace in the rack. When she settled back in the pew and crossed her legs, her skirt rose above her knee and I saw the hem of her slip peeking out from under the skirt. Out of the corner of my eye I thought I saw her watching me.

Then Reverend Swaim launched into our multitude of sins, laying as much blame on Eve as he could and reminding us that Eve's sinning is passed along through the act of sexual intercourse. His words were a monotonous metronome of morality. After a few minutes, I tuned him out, emptied my mind of sin and inhaled Pam Merkel's aromas while my eyes followed a beam of sunlight streaming through the stained glass windows onto her lap, a beam of rose sunlight that seemed to be drawn to the diamond ring on her finger. When she shifted her hand, a flash of sunlight reflected from the diamond, catching me in the eye. I closed my eyes, wondering if the women visiting the salesmen in the motel rooms at the General left their wedding rings in their parked cars. I started to doze off when I saw a woman's hands tucking her wedding ring into the glove compartment of her car, snapping the glove compartment shut then reaching her hand to her hair to pat it in place as she looked at herself in the rear view mirror of the car. Then I realized the eyes in the mirror were Pam Merkel's. She stepped out of the car with her purse in her hand. When she got to the garage door she looked carefully in all directions before trotting across the parking lot to the door of one of the motel rooms. She knocked, then disappeared through the doorway.

I was lying on the bed when she entered the room. She shut the door behind her, locked it, then turned around to face me. She dropped her purse on a chair by the door and walked slowly towards me, her eyes fastened on mine. Inches beyond my reach, she waited while Reverend Swaim's voice rang out the far away hollow syllables.

"Concupiscence," he was saying.

"Can you undo this?" she was asking, touching the pearl buttons of her blouse. "Or do you want to watch me undress?"

"Both," I said, pulling myself to a sitting position.

She unfastened the first pearl button of her blouse and slowly the second, then let her hands drop to her sides. The buttons slipped magically away as I touched each one. I stood and pulled her blouse open and off her shoulders, then tossed it onto the bed. I kissed her shoulders and neck while I reached around behind her and unzipped her skirt and let it fall to the floor. She sat down on the edge of the bed, kicked off her high heels and pulled her slip up over her garter belt while she unfastened her hose and curled them down her legs. I reached down and took the hem of her slip and pulled it up and over her head. She put her arms behind her back and unfastened her bra and pulled it off and flung it across the room and lay back with her head on the pillow. I kneeled beside her and took hold of her panties and slipped them off. She opened her arms and legs to me and the organ blared and I felt an ecstatic explosion in my spinal column and pulsating in my pants as Pam Merkel's hand reached across me, reached to open the glove compartment for her ring which wasn't there because we were on the east end, the church end, of Riggles Creek Drive, not the west end of the General Jackson motel, and the organist was playing and Pam Merkel's hand, wearing her wedding ring, lifted the hymnal from the rack on the back on the pew. She stood and opened the hymnal and held it for her husband, for the two of them as they sang together, their voices lifting towards heaven.

I rose up from my seated afterglow to a standing position and mouthed the words of the hymn. Midway through the hymn, Pam Merkel turned and gave me a look as though I was singing so far off key I might as well be singing some other song. Did she know? I glanced down at my pants. Thankfully I had worn navy blue slacks. The blue might just get darker and it wasn't showing, yet.

The collection plate was passed down the pew and I emptied my wallet into it, all twelve dollars. We sang another hymn, "Oh God Our Help In Ages Past" (that one I do remember) and then came the benediction that I thought would never end. As the organist hit the chord for the recessional, everyone stood to exit but me. I leaned forward with my head bowed over my pants while the attendees shuffled their feet and moved toward the exit. I felt Pam Merkel's hand touch my shoulder. I glanced up from my prayerful pose and gave her a weak smile.

"It was so good seeing you," she whispered. "I hope to see more of you in the future."

"Yes, see more of me," I mumbled. "I hope so, too."

She turned to leave and I closed my eyes and gave thanks for the miracle I had experienced: I had brought forth seed without ever touching myself or another person.

When most of the congregation had made their way out, I stood and buttoned my jacket. I hoped it would cover the evidence. As I walked up the aisle, I imagined the eyes of those lingering at the church door focusing directly on my pants. Reverend Swaim was standing at the doorway still shaking hands with the last few members of the congregation. There was no way to get by him without stopping to shake his hand, so I got in line and began to rehearse everything I could possibly say to him.

"So good to see you back in attendance," he said when it was my turn. He took my hand in both of his, his face beaming like he'd just sold me a piece of used furniture he was about to give away. "I hope your studies are going well. By the way, I noticed you looked so intent today. My message must have struck a chord."

"I felt quite moved," I told him.

"And last I looked," he said approvingly, "you were still deep in prayer."

A perverse part of me wanted to tell him I'd held the reins of the devil. But I couldn't do that to him. "I've been away so long there was much catching-up to do," I finally managed.

"Yes, I suppose so," he replied with a touch of surprise. "Well, I do hope we'll see you again next Sunday."

"Next Sunday? I don't know what I'm doing next Sunday."

"Perhaps someday then," he said as his chin dropped with disappointment.

I tried to say something religiously helpful to him, but I don't think it came out the way I meant. "Wasn't Eve following a plan?"

Reverend Swaim looked up, his eyes blinking like something might be clicking somewhere in his head. A gust of wind blew through the open doorway of the church and lifted his thin combed-over hair straight up. "Have a nice day," he said shaking my hand. Reverend Swaim turned away and walked back into the dark interior of his church.

As I stepped out into the light of the front porch of the church, I felt like I could soar off into the clear blue sky. The air smelled fresh and the sunshine felt like the warm hand of God on my back. When I got to the car and turned to look back at the church with its pointed arch and tall steeple, it looked like a giant toy, one of the buildings from my model train set I packed away many years ago.

The Silver Streak started with the first crank and the

engine hummed like a beehive. I sat there listening and thought about Curtis always tinkering with his own car's engine and never quite getting it right. He didn't get Pam Merkel right either. Even if his gossip were true, Curtis would never understand that Pam Merkel was really doing God's work.

Stonewall Jackson's Saddle

I'd seen Stonewall Jackson's favorite horse, Little Sorrel, in the basement of one of those grey stone buildings at the Virginia Military Institute in Lexington. The horse was, of course, stuffed. In a glass case, the horse didn't look like a war mount—just kind of scrawny and weather-beaten. He was there because Jackson had been a professor at VMI and because people thought Jackson was a military genius (right up there with Alexander the Great and Hannibal, according to my high school history teacher). I read that Jackson's horse lived to be thirty-six years old and had been paraded all over the South in the years after the Civil War. Little Sorrel was even a main feature at the World's Fair in New Orleans in 1885, and my great-grandmother claimed to have a bracelet made from hairs clipped from his tail. I guess if you lose big like the South did, you need all the heroes you can get. Even four-legged ones.

I never knew anything about Stonewall Jackson's saddle until the day an old horse trainer named Charlie Arnaberry told me about it. I've mentioned Arnaberry before. He had a stable a few miles down the road from Mr. Hamlyn's farm. Arnaberry boarded and trained horses, but he made his real money selling horses. He had as good a reputation as a horse trader could have. That is, he never sold anyone a horse that didn't suit them. At least that's what people said about him. I rode for Arnaberry from time to time when his back was giving him trouble and he couldn't exercise horses himself. He had a couple of other fellows who worked for him, but they weren't riders. If Charlie was really hard up for help and couldn't find somebody to ride for him, I'd skip school and take the job. I never told my mom I was skipping school. She wouldn't understand that I'd learn more about the real world from Charlie than from my teachers. I'd hang around after I'd ridden the horses that needed work and listen to Charlie's stories. They always got better after he started hitting the bottle, which he claimed he only did to ease his back pain. And like most hardworking gentlemen, he kept the bottle out of sight. Charlie could tell a story with such a straight face, I never knew whether he was giving me the real facts or making it all up. Maybe he didn't know either.

One day after Charlie had been out to his car to take a couple of pulls off a pint of bourbon he kept under the front seat, we started talking about the Civil War and who were the best generals. I told Charlie that some history teachers consider Stonewall Jackson to be among the top three generals of all time. Then Charlie started telling me about this old saddle—Stonewall Jackson's saddle. Charlie said he had even touched the saddle, rubbed his hands over it. He described the saddle in detail just like he had looked at it the day before. He told me it had a high pommel and cantle and well-worn roll pads. The saddle had never deteriorated and over a hundred years later it was still in remarkable condition, according to Charlie. It had been handed down through various owners over the years and all had seen to it that the saddle was regularly soaped and occasionally oiled with neat's-foot oil (made from boiling down feet, skin and shin bones of cows).

"That leather was still pliable," Charlie said, giving his head a little shake of admiration.

"No way. Not after a hundred years," I said.

"It was. Just goes to show you if you take care of something it'll last. You could tell it was old, mind you. It had a deep walnut stain, almost black. It didn't have a girth on it. Long gone, I reckon. Hard to keep up with girths anyhow. But the stirrups and stirrup leathers were the originals. Stirrups made out of iron, not steel. And the stirrup cover on the left side had a bloodstain on it that would never come out, and you couldn't cover it up, they told me. Jackson had been riding in the saddle the night his own troops shot him out of it. Guess that stain was proof of it right there. A little hard to see that blood spot at first because the saddle is awful dark. But it was there alright," Charlie said.

"You see it over in Lexington?"

"Nope. I don't remember where I saw it. They told me some family living near Fredericksburg got hold of the saddle right after Jackson was shot. How they did this is a mystery. Must have been worth a pretty penny if it was the real thing, I mean Stonewall Jackson's saddle—that's a relic." Charlie stood up and stretched, then he grabbed his back right down at the hinge. "Got to get something out of the car," he said.

I knew he was going to go take another drink. He didn't like to drink in front of me. And he never drank in front of any of his customers, but he wasn't very good at hiding what he was doing. Everybody knew about that pint of bourbon wrapped in a brown paper bag under the front seat of his car. And you could pick up that syrupy whiskey smell ten feet away from him when he'd come back into the barn.

"Something else about that saddle of Jackson's," Charlie said when he walked back into the tack room where I was cleaning a saddle. "They tell me that putting it on the back of even the most unruly horse would quiet it as soon as the girth was cinched. And when your boots slip into the stirrups, you feel like you're in command of everything in sight. That's what they said."

After Charlie told me the story with me taking it all in like he was some walking encyclopedia, he laughed like he'd had a good joke on me. But the way he kept his eye on me when he laughed left me believing he was on the fence about the saddle himself. So I kind of believed him. I think he might have wanted to believe the whole story, but the manly role was to act skeptical, distance himself from another one of those tall tales horse people tell.

One afternoon not long after Charlie Arnaberry told me about Jackson's saddle, I was in the Old Dominion Pawnshop on Jefferson Street looking for a deal on a set of drums. I'd always wanted to play drums and the price for a new set was ridiculous, definitely outside my skimpy budget. I knew the pawnshop owner, a roly-poly guy named Toby. I'd pawned a few things there whenever times got really tight. And when I had money, I was always looking for deals.

So Toby, he said to me, "Hey, you ride horses, don't you?"

"Yeah, I do."

"Some old guy left a saddle here and he never came back for it. His time's up on the tab," Toby said. "Guy claimed it was a Civil War saddle, like the Johnny rebs used to ride in. Make you a deal on it." He sucked on his cigar and watched me.

"Civil War saddle? Right." I gave him one of my "okay-why-not" shrugs.

So we went to the back of the shop, back past hocked radios and fishing gear and toolboxes of all sizes, lawnmowers, a Naugahyde easy chair, racks of roller skates until we got to this pine sea chest.

"This thing's a treasure. Been keeping it safe," Toby said, stuffing the cigar into his mouth and bending over the chest. He opened it and pulled out something covered in a moth-eaten blanket. Then he unwrapped an ancient looking saddle and held it up with one hand while he took his cigar out of his mouth with the other. "A hundred fifty bucks and it's yours. I'll even tie a ribbon on it for you."

"A hundred fifty bucks for that old piece of leather that wouldn't even make a dog's chew-toy?" That's always the first sort of thing you say to a pawnbroker like Toby. Makes them think you're not interested. But they know the ropes. They expect you to knock whatever they've got.

"Let me take it out in the light," Toby said.

"Don't bother," I told him.

But he walked out to the front of the shop and set the saddle down on a shelf in the show window. He studied his cigar, then found a big glass ashtray for it. He pulled out his handkerchief and wiped the dust off the saddle. Then he reintroduced it to me with a grand sweep of his hand. "There it is. A piece of history. Like I said, this old guy told me it was a civil war saddle. Something about belonging to a famous general. A rare antique. Even got a brand on it. See, right here—says CSA. What do think that stands for? Confederate Soldiers of America."

"Confederate States of American," I said, correcting him.

"That's exactly what I mean. Come to think of it, I priced it too low."

"If the South had won it might be worth something, Toby."

"If the South had won I wouldn't be standing here. And, by the way, you're standing on conquered ground. You ever think of that?"

Toby had a New Jersey accent and was always ready to let fire some sarcastic comment like that. Yankees can't help it.

I thought about the story Charlie Arnaberry had told me, but I just glanced at the saddle. "Yeah, yeah, every old thing is a museum piece, Toby. I'm looking for drums, not antiques."

"Got no new drums." He blew a speck of dust off the saddle. Then he picked up his cigar and relit it. He took a big draw and let the smoke rise over his head. "A little shoe polish on this thing and it'll look like a classic," he said. "I ought to sell it to the Smithsonian." Then he picked a piece of tobacco off the tip of his tongue, studied it a moment and flicked it away. "Tell you what I'll do. Take it for sixty-five and I'll call you when I get a set of drums. You'll be the first to hear."

The saddle fit Arnaberry's description but there must have been thousands of Civil War saddles, although they all rotted away years ago. Without looking too closely at the saddle and having Toby thinking I had any interest in it, I was trying to see if there was a bloodstain on the left stirrup cover. Sure enough, there seemed to be a big teardrop shape that had a slightly different hue—rusty looking against the walnut-brown leather.

"Twenty-five," I told him.

Toby shook his head. He picked up the saddle and headed to the back of the store.

"Thirty," I called out to him.

Toby stopped, turned around and said, "Oh what the

hell. We're friends. I'll take forty."

It was definitely an antique saddle and somebody had taken good care of it before it ended up in a chest in the back of the pawnshop, but I still walked out of there carrying the saddle and cursing myself for having been taken in by Toby—and Arnaberry's story. Sure there was something authentic about the saddle, but anybody who ever heard the story could have doctored up that leather stirrup cover to make it look like it had a drop of blood on it. "Damn thing isn't worth more than fifteen bucks if it's worth a nickel," I grumbled to myself as I set the saddle into the trunk of my car.

When I got home I took the saddle into the house and went over it with a magnifying glass looking for any marks identifying manufacturer, anything that could give me a clue to the date it was made. But I guess it was a custom made saddle for the CSA. Or somebody had stamped that mark on the leather at a later date. I measured the seat at fifteen inches. It was deep and had a comfortable feel to the pommel and cantle. The stirrup irons looked old and they weren't stainless steel, maybe iron. I took some glycerin saddle soap and tried to wash that teardrop stain off the leather but it wouldn't clean off. The saddle was old but it couldn't be over a hundred years old, I told myself.

When I showed it to my mom and told her it was a Civil War saddle, she just shook her head and said, "I don't know beans about saddles but shoe leather only lasts about forty years. You didn't spend good money on that old thing, did you?"

"No, it was bad money, Mom. But I got myself a good conversation piece." I was already thinking about taking it over to Arnaberry's stable and telling him I found Jackson's saddle. In fact, I'd get Charlie to try it out on a horse I knew he was having some problems with. I'd have my joke on him.

The old man had a reputation for working miracles on horses and most of it he did from the ground. People said he could turn any horse, even a real problem horse, into something suitable for any rider. I'd helped out at his stable enough to know his technique. He'd rig up a bridle with elastic reins that connected to a surcingle to make a bitting harness, as he called it. He'd put it on a horse and let him wear it in the stall, and then Charlie would lunge the horse every day with this bitting rig. He didn't get on the horse's back until the horse was off the bit. "The first thing you do is get the horse's mouth right," Charlie always said. "Then you talk to them with your hands."

A few months back he'd made what he thought was a slick purchase on a new horse. It was a seven-year old gelding he bought off the tracks in Maryland. The lady he got the horse from said her cousin's family had raced the horse in Ireland and then brought him back to Maryland and got a few more miles out of him. Charlie told me he bought him for almost nothing. The horse's racing days were over, but I know Charlie was thinking he could get the horse to settle down, teach him that running wasn't his job anymore, get him jumping nice and steady and turn a good profit on him. He was a handsome horse, well muscled with a proud look about him. A pretty color, too, bright-red chestnut with a star on his face and two half-stockings. He stood about sixteen-three hands tall. Charlie called him Don Juan. The horse had a smart look in his eyes: he looked sensible, but we soon realized why Charlie had gotten him so cheaply. You'd be riding him along and everything would be going fine, then for no reason at all he'd stop and start backing up. And he wouldn't stop backing no matter what you did. A whip didn't faze him. I might as well have been swatting flies off his butt with it. One day I rode Don Juan out on the trail and he stopped for no reason then started backing. He didn't stop until we got all the way back to the stable. I didn't know a horse could back up for an eighth of a mile but his horse sure did it, sort of crab-stepping all the way.

Charlie and I tried everything we knew to get Don Juan going right. I'd be on the horse and Charlie would be riding another horse, and when Juan stopped, Charlie would keep on going. Horses don't like to be left behind but this horse would just stand still for a few moments with his ears sort of going out to the side like they were seeking direction signals, then he'd get into reverse gear and away we'd go—backwards. No way to stop him until he stopped himself. I tried spurs. We changed Don Juan's bit a dozen times. I got a longer whip. Nothing.

The next day I had free—it was on a Saturday—I drove over to the stable with the old saddle. I showed it to Charlie who didn't say anything except, "Well it's old. That's for sure. I don't know if it's a Civil War saddle or not. Hope you didn't pay much for it."

"Well, you said you'd touched it. Is this it? This Jackson's saddle?"

"I couldn't say for sure."

"Think you can find a girth that would work on it? Put the saddle on Don Juan. We've tried everything else."

Charlie sat there thinking for a minute or two then he turned the saddle over and looked at the fittings for the girth. "I might have something that'll work. I reckon these fittings will hold."

I groomed Don Juan while Charlie poked around in the tack room hunting up a girth. I told the horse I had a special treat for him. Charlie finally found an old girth he thought would work. Then I saddled up Don Juan. As soon as I set the saddle on his back, the horse turned his head around to look at it; his ears pricked forward, his nostrils starting to flare and his eyes seemed to get bigger and rounder. I thought to myself, well damn, this thing's freaking him out. But I cinched it up anyway and let the stirrup leathers out to my length. "I must be taller than Stonewall or whoever else's been riding in it," I told Charlie.

I put the bridle on Don Juan and led him out of the stable and into the riding ring. The horse didn't just walk outside, he pranced out into the sunlight like he was getting ready to run in the Derby. I had to take a good hold of the reins to keep his feet on the ground.

"Damn, he's full of himself today," Charlie said as he helped take hold of the horse's bridle so I could mount up.

I barely got my left toe in the stirrup before the horse bolted. I mean he took off, whipping the reins out of Charlie's hands and knocking my ass on the ground. And there was no catching that horse. He tore around the ring a couple of trips at a full gallop with Charlie yelling "whoa boy, whoa boy" and cursing about his reins getting stepped on. The next trip around the ring, the horse sailed over the fence at the far end and went galloping out the lane toward the highway.

Charlie was cursing up a storm. "Son-of-a-bitch is gonna get killed in the road!"

We watched the horse galloping for the highway, cars coming from either direction. I couldn't look until I heard Charlie mutter, "Thank God."

I opened my eyes to see Don Juan ripping through a cornfield on the other side of the highway and heading for the far hills. We hopped into Charlie's car to try to chase the horse down.

"I thought Jackson's saddle was supposed to quiet a horse," I said.

"Must be the wrong damn saddle," Charlie muttered.

"Maybe he'll stop and back on home," I suggested.

Charlie just glared at me.

We headed in the general direction the horse was

running, following whatever roads would take us in that direction. Beyond the cornfield was a big open hayfield and beyond that the creek.

"Maybe he'll stop when he gets to the water," I offered hopefully.

Charlie didn't say anything. He just kept driving and cursing under his breath and acting like he wanted to reach under the seat for his bottle, but he didn't. We went up and down a few gravel roads and drove up to a couple of farmhouses but didn't see any sign of the horse or anybody standing in the yard waving at us. In a few more minutes we saw a cop car. "Somebody must have called the police, so that means he's gone past some houses down near Meachum's Crossing," Charlie allowed. Good thing it was a rural area, mostly farmland all around, just a few houses clustered here and there. We stopped and asked a guy on a tractor if he'd seen a horse run by. He had. He pointed out the direction it went. Charlie and I drove on out the road the farmer pointed to, Church Creek Hollow Road it's called. After about a mile we got to the old country church that gave the road its name.

When we drove by the church, which was on my side of the road, I saw the horse. He was standing quietly under a tree beside the church just as though somebody had ridden him there and stepped inside for the morning service. And the saddle was gone! Charlie pulled the car into the church parking lot and we got out and went over to the horse. We talked softly to him so he wouldn't spook and run away again. But that horse wasn't going anywhere. He was winded, wet, and lathered and he just stood there with his head hanging low. Charlie walked up to the horse and looked him over. "Not a scratch on the son-of-a-bitch! And no saddle! And would you look at that? I can't believe he didn't break those reins. Look at 'em! They're laying across his neck just like somebody dropped them there."

Charlie picked up each one of the horse's feet to see if the horseshoes were still holding and make sure he hadn't injured himself after all that running over the countryside. "Son-of-a-bitch looks fine. You hang onto him and I'll go get the trailer," Charlie said.

"How about if I ride him back?" I offered.

"Bareback? On this crazy son-of-a-bitch?"

"He's worn out. Doesn't look to me like there's any running left in him. I'll try to figure out which way he came. Look for the saddle on the way back. Just give me a leg up."

"You're welcome to try. But that crazy thing just might start backing up. You'll be right back here at the church."

"On the other hand, he might have learned his lesson and wants to get back to the stable," I said, giving a Don Juan a reassuring pat.

Well, Don Juan didn't back up on the way to Charlie's stable. He walked as quietly as a draft horse after a day of plowing. Along the way, I started thinking about Lockett and wondered if she still rode bareback. There's something to be said for direct contact with a horse. But I wouldn't do it naked.

When we got to the highway, Charlie was there talking to the police officer, the same one who must have gotten a call about the runaway horse. The cop stopped the traffic and Don Juan and I paraded across the road. I halfway expected him to take that opportunity to stop and start backing again. But he didn't. In fact, he never backed up again as far as I know. Over the next few weeks I rode him in the ring and on the trail and he did fine, as quiet and steady as you'd ever want a horse to be. Charlie eventually found a buyer for the horse and he said he never got any complaints about Don Juan's behavior. No more backing up. His new owners told everyone they had gotten this push-button horse from Charlie Arnaberry. A steal, they said, and they were right about that.

As for the saddle, I never found it and Charlie said he never wanted to see it again anyhow. I think watching that horse gallop across a highway ripping his way through the traffic was almost too much for Charlie. He said his heart jumped up into his throat and he liked to never get it settled back in place. Charlie did give me forty dollars to cover the loss of my saddle. Of course, I'd rather have the saddle.

I hiked back and forth a half dozen times over every possible route Don Juan could have run and never saw the saddle. One day I did run across the same farmer on his tractor that Charlie and I had seen when we were looking for Juan. I waved him down and he cut his tractor off. I asked him if the horse still had a saddle on him when he ran by.

"Must have," he said. "They were moving on like there was no tomorrow."

"What do you mean—*they* were moving on? Wasn't but one horse."

"Well, horse and rider, you know."

"He didn't have a rider on him."

"Well, must not have been the same horse," he said and cranked his tractor engine up again.

When I got back to the stable, I told Charlie what the guy on the tractor had said.

Charlie just sat there for a long time gazing off into the distance and then he started giving his head a little shake. "Excuse me," he said. "I gotta go get something out of the car."

The Lodge

We were lucky. In our neighborhood one of the parents, Mrs. Bonny Gilwall, enjoyed being part of our scene as well as hostess for our weekend festivities. Other parents seemed to want to keep a safe distance from their kids once they had metamorphosed into teenagers. But not Miz Bonny.

She and her daughter, Cheryl, might have passed for sisters with Miz Bonny coming off as the overwhelmingly dominant older sister. Both had reddish brown hair and blue-green eyes and presented a sort of southern genteel charm. But Cheryl, I thought, had too much of her father in her to ever develop her mother's good-natured hospitableness. Cheryl did have a sweet smile and freckles like her mom. But she couldn't turn on the charm and conviviality the way her mom did.

We all called the Gilwall's house "The Lodge." Actually somebody called it that one night; we all laughed and the name stuck. If you didn't have a date there was always the Lodge. Or even if you had a date you could still go by the Lodge to see what was happening.

Cheryl's mom was the Lodge hostess. To all of us she was "Miz Bonny." Simply calling her Bonny would not have shown the respect due an adult and "Mrs. Gilwall" just didn't seem right for a woman who wore tight-fitting jeans none of the other mothers would have (or could have) worn. And "Auntie Bonny" sure as hell wouldn't have worked. So Miz Bonny, it was.

I never actually took Cheryl out on a formal date but we were close friends and schoolmates on the same social path—wherever that was going. Like some of the other girls I knew, she took riding lessons at Mr. Hamlyn's farm and we sometimes rode together. Cheryl even had her own one stall stable out behind her house where she kept a little mare named Butterbells.

One cold rainy winter night when the Lodge was not its usual beehive of activity, I sat on the sofa with Cheryl watching TV. She had a blanket pulled over her legs and she spread it over my legs as well. Eventually our hands met in the darkness of the blanket and she took my hand and placed it in her lap, warming it, nudging it closer and closer to where it wanted to be which was between her legs. If Miz Bonny had walked through the room she would never have known about the furnace we'd lit under that Tartan wool. I don't' remember what we were watching except that it was on a black and white screen and some guy was singing "Oh Happy Day." Must have been Snooky Lanson on "Your Hit Parade." Anyhow, all I could think of was bringing our hands back to my lap so Cheryl would know what she was doing to me. Eventually I got up enough nerve to inch our hands my way, crawling like two spiders back to my lap. When she touched the evidence, Cheryl smiled like she had just opened a box of chocolates. Her fingers lingered, exploring more than the fabric of my jeans, testing, honing female skills, learning what a woman could do if she sets her mind (and hand) to it. But her action was limited to biological research. Maybe keeping her eyes glued to the TV screen while her fingers did the walking wasn't so much duplicity as necessity under the circumstances. I mean, we couldn't go back to her bedroom and rip off our jeans and get to it.

The Gilwalls owned a rambling ranch style house with a two-car garage that never saw a car because a ping-pong table, a picnic table, and some retired lounge chairs took up most of the floor. Music, dancing, pennypoker or TV viewing took place in the family room. Miz Bonny was usually in the kitchen preparing something special for us, looking as busy as a chef on Thanksgiving morning.

Their house sat on a half-acre lot on a cul-de-sac in a new housing development, the lots carved by bulldozers out of the forests on the outskirts of town. The builders, as they are inclined to do, had leveled or pushed aside every living plant all the way back to where two small creeks joined, forming the major source for Riggles Creek, the almost river that our city grew around. If it had been navigable they probably would have called it Riggles River but since it was mostly rapidly rushing water over a lot of rocks they called it a creek. Tribes of Indians were said to have camped in the area, and in clearing the lot and excavating for the Gilwall's house, the rearranged earth delivered up a wealth of arrowheads.

The Gilwalls had fenced in a part of their back yard and added the stable for Butterbells. Cheryl could ford the two small creeks on Butterbells and pick up a trail through the woods that led all the way out to Mr. Hamlyn's farm. Sometimes she would ride out and take a lesson on her own horse or just trail ride with us.

If I didn't have a horseshow to go to or have a date, I would head for the Lodge. I was starting to get into ping-pong, so for me the real recreational center was the double car garage. There was an electric heater "the Fireplace" in one corner for cold weather use. But in good weather when the nights were warm, both garage doors stayed open and activity spilled out onto the paved driveway.

As I said, the family room was for dancing and some bodily contact on the sofa—always vertical, never horizontal. The room also housed the collection of Indian artifacts found in the yard and along the creek; they were Miz Bonny's treasures.

Cheryl spent most of her time on the sofa in the family room listening to records or chatting with one of her friends, or watching TV. She would sit with her legs pulled up on the sofa and her head tilted to one side in a sort of pose like the Little Mermaid statue and with a sweet far-off look in her eyes. Sometimes, when her mother was playing ping-pong in the garage, Cheryl and some lucky fellow would get wrapped up in each other's arms, eyes closed, lips connecting.

Cheryl never seemed to have a steady boyfriend, which was surprising considering all the opportunities the Lodge afforded her. But maybe there were too many guys to choose from. Maybe we were all like drones and Cheryl and Miz Bonny were the queen bees feeding us to keep us productive. (Self-centered as we were, it never occurred to us to bring food to the queens.) Like her mom, Cheryl seemed to care about everybody and had a smile for everyone, although there were times when she looked bored with the whole scene at the Lodge. What young woman wouldn't want to have some privacy so the modest necking on the sofa could really blossom into something?

Miz Bonny tried to keep a watchful eye on everything

that was going on. She would regularly breeze out of the kitchen bearing a platter of cookies or a bowl of popcorn with real melted butter (never margarine!). Since she didn't allow alcohol in the house, drinks were soft drinks or some kind of fruit punch. Occasionally somebody managed to get hold of some vodka or moonshine and spiked the punch, but not very often. Miz Bonny was on to the kids because she periodically sampled the punch. If she got a whiff of alcohol she dumped the punch and threatened to send everyone away and close up the Lodge if it ever happened again. We all knew that would have been her loss as well as ours. So the threat never took hold and alcohol continued to appear whenever someone managed to sneak some away from their parents' stash or score from one of the bootlegger's kids out past Hamlyn's farm.

Sometimes Miz Bonny would come out to the garage with a plate of cookies or brownies hot from the oven, and she'd stay to play a game of ping-pong. And always win. Miz Bonny played tennis in the local tournaments and performed well enough to get sports page write-ups that she taped onto the refrigerator door. Put a ping-pong paddle in her hand and the smiling mom-hostess became a take-no-prisoners competitor. She might go easy the first few serves to give her opponents a little encouragement, set us up, toy with her advisaries, before turning up the volley pace. The best I ever managed was four points to her eleven. Game over, the easy smile returned along with the reminder that she was not someone to mess with.

Miz Bonny had studied ballet when she was young and she loved any kind of dancing. She would dance with the guys, insisting that we needed to learn ballroom dancing and maybe a little mambo or tango. "Men who can dance will go a lot further with women," she reminded us from time to time. Then she would laugh as though trying to pass over the meaning of that remark, all the while demonstrating the importance of thigh pressure to move one's partner around the floor. She had albums of every sort of dance music and kept the family room floor free and clear and ready for action.

It was Miz Bonny who really got me into dancing. She was easy to lead and made me feel like I was something special on the dance floor. The music and the way she placed her hand on my shoulder while looking into my eyes as we swayed around the floor turned me on in a way girls never could. Girls mostly danced with girls while the boys watched or went out to the garage for ping-pong. The girls moved like bodies unwinding from too much time cramped into a school desk. But not Miz Bonny; when she danced, she could have been dropping veils (like Rita Hayworth in Salome). Cheryl would leave the room when her mom danced with me.

Mr. Gilwall worked for the Commerce Department. It was a job that kept him in Washington or often traveling to Central or South America, particularly the trouble spots. Miz Bonny allowed that the Commerce Department had many ways of keeping communism from spreading. Maybe she really meant that her husband had been doing some snooping for the government. Gilwall rarely appeared on the home scene, and when he did he looked uncomfortable, out of place with all the young people. He'd say hello, force a smile, then make a fast exit as though remembering he'd left the bathtub water running. He never played ping-pong or did any of the things his wife did. If he happened to be home, he'd be in his study or in his bedroom watching TV or playing foreign language recordings. Miz Bonny excused him from the activities saying that he was teaching himself Portuguese for his work in Brazil. He never came out, not even when a fight broke out.

Fights didn't happen all that often but whenever a

bunch of guys get together on a regular basis, something will eventually set the spark off and fists will start flying. One night when I was three points up in a good game of ping-pong, I heard the tires of a car squeal into the Lodge driveway. I glanced out of the open garage door and saw a black and white two-tone Chevy I'd never seen before. The headlights blanked, but the car kept rolling forward until it bumped my car. Under the garage floodlights I could see my car rocking back and forth. Not that any real damage could be done kissing the steel bumper of my Pontiac Silver Streak, but I was pissed-off that somebody would intentionally run into my car. And the Chevy didn't back off. It stayed bumper-to-bumper nudging the Streak. I could hear a bunch of guys in the Chevy laughing like that was somehow funny. Obviously, whoever it was wanted me to know I wasn't going to be backing out of the driveway any time soon and that there must be some subject of disagreement between us.

I couldn't recognize any faces in the Chevy. The floodlights on the garage didn't carry out that far into the driveway. One of the guys waiting his turn at ping-pong warned me the car belonged to Teddy Howlett. Oh no—trouble for sure. Howlett and his girlfriend, Stephanie Kiser, had broken up and she and I had been having lunch together in the school cafeteria. Sometimes I hung around her locker and walked her to her next class. Stephanie was cute and sassy and we had had some good laughs together in the cafeteria. I guess seeing his girlfriend enjoying herself with another guy is all Howlett needed to gather his forces for a showdown. Stephanie had warned me that Howlett was spoiled and used to getting his way and that he had a terrible temper. I wasn't worried because we were about the same size and Howlett didn't look all that athletic. He didn't play football and he wasn't on the wrestling team. I don't think the guy even ran track. Maybe he was on the bingo team.

But there were two other guys in the car with him. The one on the front seat took up a lot more space in the Chevy than Howlett. Couldn't tell about the guy in the back seat because he had a beer can in front of his face. I could hear their stupid hoots every time Howlett revved his engine, put his car into reverse, backed up then forward to nudge my car.

They must have thought they could lure me out of the security of the garage to rescue my vehicle, then teach me to respect Howlett's claim on Stephanie Kiser. Fortunately, on that particular night, I had my own support team. Well, not a team but my restless friend Curtis Peddler. Curtis had the night off from his motel job; and since he had recently broken up with his girlfriend, and his car needed more work to get it running, and he was out of beer, I brought him along to introduce him to the Lodge. It was blessed timing.

Curtis was sitting with a couple of guys trying to get a game of blackjack going for higher stakes when I stepped over to him said, "I might need your help. A little trouble outside." I nodded toward my car rocking in the driveway.

"What do you mean?"

"They've got me blocked in. Three of them—in that Chevy. Bumping my Streak, too."

"The hell you say." Curtis walked to the open garage door and looked out. Just as he did, a beer can sailed out of the car window and landed over in the yard.

Curtis weighed in at about two hundred and twenty pounds when he worked at Hamlyn's stable, but since taking the motel job and drinking beer all night he'd really put on a lot of weight, maybe up to about two fifty. And, on a dare, he'd just gotten a Mohawk haircut. With that haircut he looked like an over-stuffed Indian on the warpath. Curtis turned back to me and reached for the ping-pong paddle.

"Gimme that damn thing."

He grabbed the ping-pong paddle and headed out the door toward Howlett's car, smacking the ping-pong paddle against his butt. "Ass-whippin coming up!" he bellowed as he stomped across the driveway and grabbed a door handle on Howlett's car and gave it a tug. But they'd locked the doors when they saw Curtis stalking toward them. I followed Curtis but gave him plenty of space to do his thing.

"You boys ever had an ass-whippin?" Curtis bellowed. They all stared at Curtis as though he was something that just escaped from the zoo or maybe the penitentiary, or both. Howlett had shut off the engine in hopes, apparently, that his two companions would jump out and take care of the menace. But his companions stayed put as Curtis made his way around the car jerking on each door handle and pounding on the roof. "Come on out of there, you sissy sons-of bitches!" he roared. After circling the car, he sat down on the hood of Howlett's car and started smacking the ping-pong paddle against his open hand. "Come on you chicken-shit worthless bastards! One at a time or all three! I'm ready for some action!"

At that point neither Howlett nor his buddies were about to even crack open a window enough to yell some threats and curse words at Curtis. Surely, I thought, they couldn't rush away from one guy with a ping-pong paddle without a promise of a future reckoning. I was eating this up. I walked up to the car and stared in at them. All three sat stone-faced and silent as Curtis started bouncing his full weight up and down on the hood, rocking it, singing, "Rock a bye babies/in this piece of shit." When he jumped down from the hood and leaned over to the left front tire, Howlett must have thought Curtis was pulling out a knife to slash the tires. Somehow Curtis managed to unscrew the valve cap from the front tire before Howlett could get his engine going and into reverse and get out of the driveway. As the car squealed rubber down the street, Curtis stood in the yard of the Lodge holding up the valve cap. Then he threw it into the air and whacked it away with the paddle. He picked up the beer can lying in the grass and walked back to the garage and dropped it in the trashcan.

"What would you have done if all three of those guys had piled out of the car?" I asked him when he handed the ping-pong paddle back.

"Shit, I don't know. I figured if I couldn't bluff 'em, I'd let you settle it."

Curtis returned to the Lodge one other time with me. That was one of the few nights the police were ever called to the Lodge. A neighbor up the road had complained about the loud music. It was a warm night and all the windows and doors were open so the music did carry a long way off.

Miz Bonny turned the music down and took the cops back to the kitchen and gave them chocolate chip cookies right out of the oven. She told them, or maybe they sniffed it out, that she didn't allow drinking on the premises. They were so pleased to see well supervised teenagers that when they left they didn't even realize Curtis had taken the hubcaps off their squad car while they were in the kitchen munching cookies while investigating the disturbance. Miz Bonny gave the cops some extra cookies to take with them. Everybody came out of the Lodge and waved goodbye to them as they drove off. The police must have figured that the cul-de-sac house offered a safe place for kids to have a good time without booze so they never bothered Miz Bonny again. They didn't even come back looking for their hubcaps. I found all four of them the next morning behind the front seat of the Silver Streak. A few days later I was driving by the Goodwill center so I stopped and donated the cop car hubcaps. The guy at Goodwill I handed them to said, it was the first time they had ever gotten hubcaps in such good shape.

"Almost new," I told him.

On another night, when Curtis wasn't along for the fun, a warm balmy spring night when the garage doors were wide open and the sweet humid air of springtime was settling in and all should have been just right with the world, I got into a brawl with a kid named Ronald. This guy didn't go to Jubal Anderson High and until that night I'd never seen him before. From the moment Ronald strolled through the open doorway of the garage with a lit cigarette in his hand and a look on his face like he wanted to be voted homecoming king but didn't think he'd bother to accept it, I knew there was going to be trouble. But I didn't know that I was going to be the cause of it. Marvin Slusser, who brought Ronald along with him to the Lodge, introduced him to all of us, but there was no attempt on Ronald's part to register with anyone, no eye contact, nothing. He just stood there inside the doorway pumping smoke out of his mouth and glancing around at Marvin like—okay, so where's the action? The way he dangled his arm and held his cigarette at his side and lightly tapped ashes on the floor got me riled before Ronald ever opened his mouth.

"Flick your ashes outside, man, this is a house," I told him.

"Looks like a garage to me," Ronald answered looking up at the unfinished ceiling.

From that instant on we were like two male dogs bristling and pissing and scratching the ground although I had made a halfway attempt at first to give civility a try. I invited Ronald to put out his cigarette and play a game of ping-pong.

"Chink-sport?" Ronald sneered.

"Good for hand-eye coordination. Might help you if

you want to play baseball someday ... when you grow up." I told him.

"Marvin, you didn't tell me this place was full of smart asses," Ronald announced with a glance at his friend.

"Hey, you—take that damn cigarette out in the street and suck on it."

Ronald took a deep draw and blew a few smoke rings in my direction. Then he blew one up in the air and stuck his middle finger through it.

"I said get the damn cigarette out of here."

Ronald cocked his head and sneered. Then he took a big pull on his cigarette, leaned my way and blew smoke.

I dropped my paddle and boiled around the table after Ronald who took a few steps back out into the driveway, flipped away his cigarette and put up his fists. From the way he got onto his toes and guarded his chin I realized this guy knew something about boxing. But so did I, because my dad was into boxing and we had a speed bag and a body bag in our garage and I had taken some boxing lessons at the YMCA. We both started swinging and I managed to land a couple of good punches before he got me a solid one. Then we backed off and circled each other, fists up and snarling.

"Let him have it, Ronald," Marvin yelled and Ronald swung and missed. Then I caught him right in the mouth and he kind of went crazy and started swinging wildly and I was just trying to block some of the punches. The guys standing around us were cheering us on. Suddenly Miz Bonny charged into the melee screaming, "Break it up! Break it up!" We stopped like the bell had rung ending the round.

"You!" she yelled, pointing to Ronald who was spitting blood out of his mouth, "Out! Get out of here and don't come back! Marvin," she told the kid who brought Ronald, "remove your friend from my property and don't ever bring him back here!"

"And as for you!" she said glaring at me—I thought I was next to be ordered away—"I'm ashamed of you!" She stood there wagging her finger at me and shaking her head before pulling me into the bright lights of the garage. "You're bleeding! Let me take a look at that cut on your head!"

Ronald had landed a solid punch just above my right eye and blood was running down the side of my face.

Miz Bonny grabbed my hand and pulled me all the way to the bathroom. She closed the door. And locked it. She reached into the closet and grabbed a washcloth and held it under the coldwater tap. She wrung it out and handed it to me saying, "Use this. Try to keep the blood off your shirt. Better still, take your shirt off." I held the washcloth on my head and she unbuttoned my shirt and pulled it loose and over my shoulders. She tossed it over the shower curtain rod and had me sit on the edge of the bathtub while she washed her hands.

"I can't believe you of all people would get into a fight. And here at my house," she said, drying her hands while giving me another hard look.

"I can't believe he hit me like that," I said. "Never saw it coming. He must be left-handed. Blinded me with his footwork, too. I don't know ... "

She studied the wound a moment, then she got out a first aid kit from her closet and took out a package of gauze pads. She started to rip open the package but stopped to wash her hands again. "My father was a doctor and he insisted that doorknobs harbored almost as many germs as money."

"Money's dirty?"

"Filthy."

"I'll never touch it again," I told her.

"Hush," she said as she wiped away the blood with the gauze pad and pressed on the cut to try and stop the bleeding. "I may have to take you to the emergency room. This is deep."

"Can you see my brains?"

"Do you have any?"

"Only one. It's very small."

"I'll say."

"Just put a band-aid on my head and it'll be all right."

"Maybe. I'm going to clean this off with some hydrogen peroxide. It won't hurt. Just bubbles. Close your eyes and lean your head over this way," she said, tilting my head over the tub. She leaned over me pouring and dabbing peroxide on my right eyebrow with a gauze pad in one hand and the bottle of peroxide in the other.

When she stopped pouring and I opened my eyes I was looking right down the gaping open neck of her very loose fitting blouse. And she wasn't wearing anything underneath.

"Getting a good peek, are you?"

"It's helping me get my mind off the pain," I offered, trying to sound embarrassed and grateful all at once.

"You probably want to do more than just look?"

"What do you mean?"

"Don't you want to touch?" she asked in the same tone as if she were offering me a molasses cookie.

I didn't know what to say. Of course I wanted to touch her breasts but I couldn't say that. Nor could I say—"Oh no Ma'am, reckon I'd better not." Finally, I managed, "Actually my hand hurts worse than my head. I might have broken it. It doesn't seem to be working. Fingers are numb."

"Then reach up under my blouse and see if they still work."

"What?"

"Your hand. You'll be surprised how much it helps."

"My hand!"

"Yes."

"Where?'

"Wherever you want."

"Are you serious?" I asked.

"If you need to, go ahead."

"I can't do that!" The thought of Cheryl sitting in the family room on the sofa eating popcorn with Buzzy Edmunds while I fondled her mother's breasts was too much. But after a moment's reflection that this was a once-in-a-lifetime opportunity, I reached up inside her blouse and explored the soft curvature of her breast. My hand cupped her breast sending joy all the way up my arm into my addled brain, completely redirecting all the nerve impulses. Then, trying to make light of what I was doing, I offered, "You're right. It's a miracle. Pain's gone." (And it really was.)

Miz Bonny kept to her first aid task as though my hand had been cupping her elbow. "Do you do that with my daughter?" she quietly asked.

"Cheryl's never tried to put my head back together," I said, taking my hand away.

"You know what I mean."

"But you told me to."

"What if she told you to?"

I didn't answer at first. Finally I said, "I guess I would if she told me to do it."

"Oh, you're such a bad boy."

"Bad? Just being obedient. Doing what I'm told to do."

"Obedient my fanny. You're just putty. And I'd better *never* hear of that with Cheryl. If I .... " She let whatever that 'if' was go and dried the wound with another gauze pad and carefully taped the gaping skin together. "You need to have somebody look at that tomorrow. Promise me you'll do that." She stepped back and studied the taping on my eyebrow.

"I will," I said. I stood up and leaned over and kissed her softly on the cheek. "Thank you."

She drew back and stared at me as though I was out of focus, her hand touching my chest. Then to my surprise, she slid her hand down to my waist and around my back as she leaned into me, closed her eyes and kissed me on the lips. I put my arms around her and held onto that wonderful kiss as long as I could, until she pushed my arms down and stepped back.

"Don't you ever say a word about this to anyone."

"I won't."

"I know you won't. Now put your shirt on and get out of here."

She watched me fumble with the shirt buttons, but I was flustered and the fingers on my right hand were swelling so fast from hitting Ronald's thick head they didn't want to do buttons.

"You really did hurt your hand."

"Would I lie to you?"

So she buttoned my shirt then unbuckled my belt and unzipped my pants just enough to carefully tuck my shirttail in. She zipped my pants back up and buckled my belt back while her eyes held mine. The two of us just stood there looking at each other, both of us trying to hold back a laugh while feeling that something had happened that wasn't intended. If I had thought of a word to say my tongue wouldn't have been able to do much with it. Finally, she gave me a little shove towards the door. "We need to get an ice pack on your hand. And your head. You're starting to grow an egg up there."

Over the next few weeks I avoided the Lodge. I wasn't sure how to face Miz Bonny and I didn't want our kiss diluted by the wrong words. Maybe it meant nothing to her, but I couldn't stop thinking about how she took care of me and what she let me do. I woke up some nights feeling like I was holding Miz Bonny in my arms, dancing with her. I wanted to be with her, touch her again. I remembered what Mr. Hamlyn had said about the restlessness of a married woman with a teenage daughter. But I went to movies instead and tried to take some lessons in coolness from James Dean.

When I did go back to the Lodge, I hung around the garage for a while. Eventually, I strolled into the kitchen. Miz Bonny looked up from her mixing bowl and gave me a quick smile. I leaned against the counter and watched silently as she poured milk into the batter she was stirring. I watched her add the chocolate chips and drop the cookie dough onto the baking sheet. After she put it into the oven and set the timer, she wiped her hands on her apron then placed them on either side of my face and pulled my forehead toward her.

"Now for a close up. Hmm—healing nicely. And no stitches! You didn't see a doctor?"

"No, the lady that put my head back together did such a good job I didn't need stitches. Perfect taping."

We stood there looking at each other for a long moment, smiling. Neither of us knew what to say next. Finally I managed, "How can I thank you? That was a wonderful thing you did for me. *All* of it."

"Good for me, too," she said and turned away to pick up the empty mixing bowl.

I stepped up behind her and put my hand on her shoulder and leaned my face close to her ear and whispered, "I really mean it." She sat the bowl down and reached her hand around to her shoulder and patted my hand but she didn't turn around and look at me. After that, whenever I visited, we always had a moment of eye contact and our smiles of a secret shared.

But I didn't visit the Lodge much anymore. Horseshows took up my weekends or I went out with girls who saw Cheryl as a rival. They had no interest in the Lodge society. I heard that it was still the place to go but whoever I was out with always had other plans, like the Candlelight Club, or somebody's party where the lights were low and parents were away. I did take my short-term girlfriend, Lydia Duncan, to the Lodge once during that time. Lydia had been the Dogwood Festival Queen and she was something of a celebrity at school and in the community. When I walked into the kitchen with Lydia and introduced her, Miz Bonny looked like she'd just been ordered to re-polish the silver. Still, she was as polite as ever. For me, it was good being at the Lodge again and smelling cookies baking and seeing everything looking just like it did the last time I was there. Later, when Lydia and I were out in the garage watching a game of ping-pong, Miz Bonny came out with a plate of warm from the oven chocolate chip cookies. She fed me one before offering them to anyone else, holding the cookie to my mouth until I had finished nibbling the last bite from her fingers. Then she turned smiling to Lydia and said, "He has a taste for the good life." She held out the cookie plate for Lydia but Lydia didn't take a cookie. She just stared at Miz Bonny.

When we left the Lodge, Lydia said, "What was *that* all about?"

"What do you mean?"

"The looks she gave me! And ... like those cookies. The way she fed you, put her fingers in your mouth. Girls' mothers don't do that!"

"What are you talking about?"

"I saw the way she looked at you and how she kept her fingers touching your lips. And you licked her fingers! And what she said—'He has a taste for the good life.'"

"She did? I did?"

"She's jealous of me!"

"Why would you think that?"

"Why? Obvious reasons!"

"No, that's just the way Miz Bonny is. She's friendly with everybody. She's one of the gang. She's not like other moms."

"That's for sure!"

Flowers For Miz Bonny

I didn't see Miz Bonny again for a long time until one day when I pulled into a gas station and I saw her two-toned Pontiac Bonneville (yes, that's why she bought it) being filled. I hopped out of my car and jogged over to greet her.

She reached out the car window and took my hand. "You never come to visit like you used to," she said, squeezing my hand and shaking her head as though I should be ashamed of myself. "Did you outgrow our party? I guess we're not in your league anymore," she teased, finally letting go of my hand. "I do hear things about you."

"All good?"

"I wouldn't say that," she grinned.

"I really miss my nights at the Lodge being with you

... and Cheryl. It's just ... well you know how it is with the girls I've been going out with."

"How could I? You don't bring them by anymore."

"I mean there's always some movie they want to see. Or a horseshow I want to see. Or a dance. And, by the way, no one can dance like you."

Miz Bonny shrugged. She stared straight ahead and nodded.

The gas station attendant had finished filling her car and came over to be paid. He glanced over at my car. "Fill it?"

"Five dollars worth of regular."

I told Miz Bonny I would stop by for a visit, but I didn't. I was going in too many directions.

I graduated in June in the class with Cheryl. At the graduation ceremony, I saw Miz Bonny in the school auditorium chatting away with some of the parents. Cheryl's dad actually showed up that day. He stood off to the side looking like he was trying to remember what language these people spoke. Miz Bonny and I hugged and I promised again I'd come to see her. But after graduation, I didn't see her again until one day almost a year later when I came home from college for spring break.

I could have spent the break at the beach like some of my friends but the redbuds were out and the grass was showing a touch of green. And I was aching to get back on a horse. I had dropped by Mr. Hamlyn's farm to say hello when I was home for Christmas. Mr. Hamlyn and I had taken a short ride together. We'd had a good laugh about the Christmas we got snowed in and how those horses had carried on. Naturally, his farm was my first stop on the way home.

But when I got there I found his stable completely empty! Not a horse or human anywhere! The tack room door stood open and not a saddle or bridle to be seen, only a few worn out horse blankets hanging on the racks.

The stable was just as it always had been, but the only life I saw was some rats darting around the feed room, probably wondering where all the oats had gone. I walked around the barn. No tractor in the tractor shed. No hay baler or mower. Even the manure spreader was gone. I walked over to the office and tried the door. Locked. But the sign over the door was still there.

I had recently seen a movie called *On The Beach* with scenes of city streets eerily emptied of life after a nuclear war. I felt like I was looking at the rural version of those scenes. I was beginning to get a little weak in the knees, so I went back inside the stable and sat down in the doorway of the tack room. I closed my eyes and breathed in the smells, which were still there—tanbark and hay, horse sweat and leather. Those aromas had me filling the barn again. Horses were back in their stalls. Moggins was limping to the far end of the stable, his manure fork in hand. Mr. Hamlyn was standing just outside the stable door greeting everyone like he was running for high public office, his teeth flashing a smile that could win votes regardless of what he stood for. I could almost hear the chorus of enthusiastic and anxious high-pitched voices of young riders, that special stable music of girls in love with horses.

I stood up and walked out of the barn and over to one of the paddocks to see if I could imagine horses back out in the pasture. Then I noticed surveyors' stakes sticking up out of the grass. So that was it!

I had known it was only a matter of time before Mr. Hamlyn's father-in-law would cut the place up, pave over the riding trails, and cover those pastures with new homes. Weyridge had to grow and those rolling fields were a developer's dream. But how could it happen so quickly? My mom had told me in a letter that Charlie Arnaberry's old stable was torn down in a week to make way for a supermarket. Charlie, she said, had moved to another stable a five miles further out of town. But Mom didn't mention anything about Hamlyn's place.

I drove out the road toward Grissom's Mill where Mom said Charlie had moved. I finally found his place down a side road. Charlie's new stable looked like he'd picked the old one up and moved it. And maybe he had. When I went inside I found Charlie in one of the stalls adjusting that bitting rig of his on a young horse.

"I wondered if you were ever going to find your way out here," Charlie said, glancing at me over his shoulder.

"Been busy, Charlie, getting educated."

"Hell, you hardly went to school while you was here. Riding my horses half the time."

"The desks were uncomfortable."

"Hey, got a horse I want to show you," he said. He snapped the side reins on the bitting harness and left the horse mouthing the bit. Charlie led me over to one of the other stalls.

"Charlie, I stopped by Hamlyn's place and there was nothing there."

"Oh yeah. Hamlyn and some car dealer got into it over the guy's wife. The guy kinda ripped up that little building where his wife had been diddlin with Hamlyn. Did it with a 16 gauge double barrel shotgun. Damn, don't you know that'd make you feel good, blasting away like that? Told the police he just wanted to scare the bastard. The judge said he'd have done the same thing. Hamlyn's wife got wind of it all and told her daddy to sell the damn farm. Hamlyn loaded up his trailer and hauled out heading west, so they tell me. Nice fella. Always liked him even if he did put on airs. I wish him all the best."

Charlie opened a stall door and when I looked in, there stood a familiar looking chestnut colored horse. Don Juan stopped munching hay and looked at me like he was trying to remember something really important.

"He didn't work out after all? They bring him back to you?"

"Hell no. They love this horse. Just boarding him while his owners are away."

"How's he doing?"

"Quiet as a lamb."

I stepped over to Juan and scratched his neck. "You remember me?"

"Get your boots and come on out and ride him while you're in town. Got another horse here you might know, a little mare." Charlie pointed out the end door of the stable. "She's out on the trail right now. Nice lady owns her. Says she knows you. Comes out to ride two or three times a week. Name will come to me in a minute."

I didn't know who Charlie was talking about and he never was good at remembering customer's names although he could name every Kentucky Derby winner going back to Man o'War and the jockey. Charlie showed me a few more horses and we chatted but I couldn't get the Hamlyn place off my mind.

"Charlie, you got a phone book here? And a phone I can use?"

"Yep. In the tack room." He pointed to the far end of the barn. "Leave a quarter on the bench."

My curiosity was getting the best of me. I went to the tack room and grabbed the phone book and thumbed through it for Accountants—Certified Public. The fifth name down was DuBeer, King and Robbins. I dialed and asked to speak to Lauren DuBeer. I had never phoned her before and didn't know if she even knew my name other than Cowboy. The receptionist told me she was busy and asked for my number so she could call back later. "This is urgent," I told her. "There's a huge fortune at stake. I have to speak with her right now."

"And who should I say is calling?"

"Cowboy," I said.

"Cowboy?"

"She'll know."

"Just a moment, please."

I waited for several moments then Mrs. Dubeer's voice came on the line. "Lauren DuBeer here. Who's calling?" she said.

As soon as my name came out of my mouth she said, "Cowboy, is it really you? What in the world are you up to?"

"I drove by Mr. Hamlyn's and the place is empty. Surveyor's stakes all over the fields. Charlie Arnaberry told me Hamlyn got run out of town."

"Where have you been?"

"Away at the school. But I'm here in town now. What happened?"

"You remember that red head who rode saddle horses at the farm? Piper Rhodes?

"I do."

"And you know how saddle horse people are such hot heads."

"Oh yeah."

"Well, her husband went after Neils with a gun. Rhodes put a lot of holes in the walls of the office but never really aimed at Neils, or so he said. Shot up all those Civil War heroes on the wall. Rhodes claimed temporary insanity. I don't think they even filed charges against him. The judge thought he'd done the honorable thing. I guess if Rhodes had shot Neils that would have been just fine. In some southern courts, he needed killin is still a legitimate defense."

"What happened to all the horses?"

"Felicia and her father owned the horses. They donated them to that girls' school, Southern Sem. They'll get a nice tax write-off. Neils just loaded that big horse of his ... Rex, and lit out for Arizona. Said he was taking over a dude ranch. Bet he's speaking with a cowpoke's accent already and got his horse in western tack. Probably changed his name again, too."

"The horse?"

"No, Neils."

"Again? What do you mean?"

"Guess you didn't know Neils Hamlyn wasn't his real name."

"No. What was it?"

"Porter Ulysses Grant Snelling," she said with a chuckle.

"You're kidding."

"I'm not."

"I think I've missed out on a lot."

"You sure have. Hey, it's tax time and I'm busier than a cockroach after a dinner party or I'd buy you lunch and tell you the whole story. Love to see you and catch up. Please give me a call next time you're in town. We'll make some plans for a ride. Maybe out at Arnaberry's place. He tells me you and he are old friends. We'll do something. Promise?"

"Yes Ma'am."

"And don't give me that 'ma'am' stuff. It ages a woman."

The phone went dead. I stood there for a few minutes trying to get my head screwed back on. Even Mr. Hamlyn's name was make-believe. Everything about the man was an invention, a total fiction! But I had to give him credit for creativity and showmanship. Roy Rogers had been Leonard Slye and he pulled off a good life.

Moggins must not have been around when Rhodes came back the second time. Moggins would have handled the situation. I wondered where he went?

When I stepped out of the tack room, I saw a woman on horseback riding toward the stable. The horse looked familiar. And in the saddle was, of all people, Miz Bonny. She was riding Cheryl's horse, Butterbells. I don't think I'd ever seen her ride before. I walked out to greet her.

"Well, what a surprise!" she said, when she saw me.

"I thought you were away at college."

"I was. Just home for spring break."

Miz Bonny hopped off her horse and gave me a hug. "Cheryl went to Florida for her spring break," she said, sounding notes of disappointment.

"Well that's where the party is," I said.

"Yeah, can't blame her really."

"Me, I'd rather be riding. You've got the right idea." I nodded at Butterbells.

Miz Bonny gave the horse a pat. "Getting too built up to ride back at our place. Still some countryside out here. We've got this horse that Cheryl doesn't want to sell and I've got some time. So here we are."

"That was going to be my next question. About Cheryl, school—how's it going for her? And how are you getting along without the gang?"

"Cheryl sounds happy," she said, leading Butterbells into the stable. "And it's quiet on the cul-de-sac these days except for all the construction going on in the neighborhood. Say, what are you doing now? Why don't you come over and let me fix you some lunch and we'll catch up on all that's been going on for ... how long now?"

"Will you play me a game of ping-pong?"

"Maybe." She gave Butterbells another pat and turned the mare over to one of Charlie's grooms.

I told Charlie I'd be back with my boots later. I got in my car and followed Miz Bonny home. When we pulled into the driveway, I was surprised to see a "For Sale" sign in the yard.

"You didn't tell me you had your house for sale," I said as we walked to the front door.

"Well, you know, Dennis is hardly ever at home." She slipped the key into the lock and gave it a twist. "That job with the Commerce Department keeps him on the move. He's away in Panama now," she sighed and pushed the door open and we went in. "It's a lot of house. We're thinking of getting something smaller, closer to downtown. And the new neighbors started complaining about the stable smells. That's another reason we moved Cheryl's horse to Charlie Arnaberry's place. Kind of sad to have that empty little stable out back here."

"Your neighbors don't like those earthy molasses-like life cycling organic odors of horse manure? What's wrong with them?" I was waxing poetic.

"I should have had you here to explain that."

"Of course it did occur to me that Cheryl might have children someday and I'd need space for the grandchildren. But ... you never know. She might marry someone and move across the country and never make it back here."

I followed Miz Bonny into the kitchen that looked the same as it always had except there were vases on the counter with no flowers. Before there had been flower arrangements all around the house and lots of potted plants in the kitchen.

She chatted on about Cheryl and her classes. "You know, it wasn't quite the beehive of activity around here that you remember. During a few months of Cheryl's senior year she had a boyfriend who chased everybody away."

"I think I know who you're talking about. Drove a red Ford. I'm surprised you didn't chase him away."

"I did." Miz Bonny shook her head. "Mistake of course. Cheryl took his side ... for a while. I know girls at some point have to challenge their moms. And she did. But she got over that guy and we're back as close as ever. Hey, I'm going to hop in the shower for just a minute. Long ride and I know I must smell like horse sweat."

"Nothing wrong with that."

"Make yourself comfortable. Then I'll fix us something to eat."

While I waited, I wandered back out to the family room, which had changed in the years since it was the grand leisure room of the Lodge. The first things I noticed were pictures of Cheryl in her graduation robe and some photos taken in her dorm at Sweetbriar. There was a recent picture of Miz Bonny on a tennis court, a tennis racket in hand, a winner's grin on her face. There were more pictures of their horse, Butterbells.

Then, for the first time ever, it struck me that there were no South or Central American artifacts in the room. No collectables on display in the entire house. There never had been. Curious that Gilwall would spend all that time working in exotic places and never bring back even a piece of pottery, or drinking vessel or ceremonial mask (not even a Mayan calendar). Maybe he never looked at art? Maybe he stayed glued to a desk? Or maybe he was up to some kind of government shenanigans and didn't want any evidence in his house. The only artifacts on display were Miz Bonny's arrowheads, dozens of them. I picked through them thinking they probably weren't used for practicing. Probably dropped out of cooked meat.

"Every time I dig in the garden I find another arrowhead." Miz Bonny' voice sounded behind me.

When I turned around, she was standing barefoot in the doorway wearing a white bathrobe and shaking out her wet hair and patting it with a towel. Her frizzled damp hair and moist skin made her look more like a roommate than a neighborhood mom.

"You've just about got a museum here," I offered, trying to be cool about the fact that she was wearing only a robe sashed loosely at the waist and that we were alone in her house for the first time ever.

"I should donate them to a museum. Nobody sees them here. Maybe I should let archeologists dig up the yard. Had to have been a camp by the creek." She shrugged and threw the towel over her shoulder and cinched her robe tighter. Then rubbing her hands together, she said, "You're probably too hungry to wait for me to dress. What would you like for lunch?"

"Anything you fix will be great, I'm sure."

She made omelets with chopped chives taken from a pot in the windowsill, the only pot with anything growing. During lunch she told me about some of the gang that she had heard about. Few bothered to get in touch with her, but she had gotten stories from Cheryl. Miz Bonny wanted to know all about my schoolwork. I told her I was thinking of majoring in biology.

"Why biology?"

"Curious about where we came from."

"You mean like from monkeys?"

"Further back."

"Fish?"

"Beyond fish. Evolution only goes back so far. I want to know about the first self-replicating living cell. How did it happen?"

"Didn't lightning strike a little puddle of choice chemicals?"

"And presto—shazam! Life! Maybe. But something's missing."

"Good luck finding it." She smiled and gave me a wink and tucked a bite of omelet into her mouth.

"And Cheryl ... has she decided on a major yet?"

"Sociology most likely. She's probably still trying to understand why her mother hosted so many kids here." Miz Bonny laughed. She didn't say anything more about Cheryl until she was moving the dishes from the table. She casually asked, "Did you and Cheryl ever ...?" She didn't complete the question; she just stopped in mid-swing to the sink with my plate in her hand, her eyes on mine.

"No. Never," I told her.

She set the dishes in the sink, then turned around and took my hand and led me back into the family room. "I don't have anybody to dance with anymore. Will you dance with me?"

"I can't wait."

She put on a record, one of those slow pieces they used to spin at proms, usually the last song of the night—"My Prayer." It was by a group called The Platters. They had turned out one smoochy-waltz hit song after another during the same time Elvis was getting us all shook up.

I kicked off my shoes and put my arm around her waist and took her hand as we swayed to the music, our feet barely moving.

"Do you appreciate me?" she asked.

"Yes."

" Just for all the cookies and popcorn?"

"For everything."

"Then why didn't you ever let me know? Send me flowers? A letter. I never expected any of the other kids to think about me." She paused a moment, pulling away and looking me in the eye, then added, "Except you."

"I thought about you a lot."

"You did?" she leaned her head against my shoulder.

"Yes. I didn't know how to ...well, you know ..."

"Never mind. Just hold me."

The record played through once and she lifted the needle back to the beginning and played it again. This time I held her even closer, burying my face in her damp hair that smelled like cucumbers and green apples. When the record finished the second time, she lifted the needle off and we continued to hold one another, still swaying, half-dancing. Then she turned her face to mine and kissed me. It was a long kiss that told me I could do anything I wanted. I reached down for the sash of her robe and pulled it loose and her robe fell open.

When her fingers began unfastening the buttons of my shirt, she said, "Seems to me I've done this before." She pulled my shirt open and tossed it away, then pressed herself against me. As we swayed to a standstill, she reached down and unfastened my belt buckle and slipped my belt off my jeans. "Cold buckle on my tummy," she said dropping the belt and unzipping me. My jeans were too tight to fall below my knees and I shook my legs trying to get them down. But they clung on to my knees and I had to push them down and take a couple of giant steps in place to pull them free. It was becoming a comic scene and I was afraid my awkwardness was destroying the mood of the moment. She never let on that she was with a boy still learning how to get out of his pants while in the arms of a woman. After the jeans, the shorts were easy.

We swayed a few more minutes before she led me back to the bedroom, leaving all my clothes on the family room floor. After we fell onto her bed, I didn't hear anything but her breathing, her whispers and murmurs, until a shrill voice called out from the doorway.

"Hi. Evie Snider here. Old Colony Realty. I let myself in with the passkey. Sorry to bother you."

I grabbed the sheet and tugged at it, pulling it over us. When I turned to look, I saw a female head of closely cropped dark hair peeking around the edge of the bedroom door.

"Listen," the voice continued, "I've got this adorable couple from New Jersey out in the car who'd love to see your house and they've only got a weentsie amount of time before they catch their flight. Is it okay if I show them around? I don't think they'll need to see the master bedroom, but if they do I'll give you a holler. I know they'll love the kitchen." She closed the door and I rolled onto my back and stared at the ceiling while Miz Bonny buried her head in the pillow laughing.

Then the head popped back through the doorway and, apparently as an afterthought, Evie Snider added, "I know you're glad to have Mr. Dilwell home. I'll just pick up his clothes in the family room if that's okay?"

She closed the door quietly. In a few moments she was back. She cracked the door, stuck her arm thru and dropped my clothes on the floor. "Here we go. All tidy out front now."

Fortunately the adorable couple from New Jersey didn't need to see the master bedroom. They must have been willing to take Evie Snider's word that it was spacious and comfortable. And currently occupied. It did take me a few moments to recover but I rekindled quickly in Miz Bonny's arms. If Evie Snider had brought the entire staff of Old Colony Realty into the bedroom we probably wouldn't have noticed.

In Virginia the month of March teases you with the promise of spring only to take it away on short notice and bring in a cold raw wind. The month was going out like a lion. I'd gotten in a couple of trail rides. I'd visited enough with the folks to assure them their hard earned money wasn't being completely wasted. And, I had reconnected with Miz Bonny. I hadn't known how to follow up on our afternoon together. I thought about writing her a long letter when I got back to school. But I couldn't just leave it at that. On my way out of town, I decided to swing by the Lodge and say goodbye in the proper way. So I drove over to a flower shop and bought half a dozen tulips, mostly reds.

Miz Bonny's Pontiac was sitting in the driveway. There was a Mercedes parked behind her car. Another real estate agent, I wondered? I pulled over to the curb just beyond the driveway and checked my watch. I couldn't stay long but I did want to see her again. I should have phoned but strange as it may seem I had not been able to say her name, to say "Bonny." She was still Miz Bonny. I didn't want to say on the phone, "Hi Mis Bonny, guess who this is."

While I sat there in my car trying to decide what to do, I wondered if maybe her husband had returned home unexpectedly. I pictured myself standing at the front door with a bouquet of flowers and Gilwall opening the door.

But in another moment I saw that it wasn't Gilwall coming out of the

front door, but a well-built man in a white dress shirt, a suit jacket and tie in his hand. The man stepped briskly to the Mercedes, pulling on the jacket. Before getting into the car, he put the tie around his shirt collar and looped it. He glanced back at the doorway he had just exited, then opened his car door and slid in. He probably wasn't there to look at the arrowhead collection. I wondered if they danced first?

The Mercedes fired up and backed out of the driveway. As his car pulled forward, the driver did a double-take when he saw me sitting in the Silver Streak at the edge of the cul-de-sac. Maybe he thought I was a low paid private eye checking up on Gilwall's wife. Or maybe he thought I was waiting my turn? He didn't brake but took his foot off the gas pedal and slowed as we eyed one another like boxers before the opening bell. Then the man mashed down on his accelerator, departing in a cloud of diesel smoke.

I picked the tulips up from the seat beside me and held them, counting them over and over. The woman at the flower shop had accidently given me seven tulips. So I plucked one from the bunch, a deep red one. As I swung the car in a u-turn on the cul-de-sac, I tossed the tulip onto Miz Bonny's yard.

Driving away, I thought how much I envied the man in the Mercedes and it wasn't for the automobile. Even though I felt a pang of jealousy, I was glad for Bonny. Then some other chamber of my brain spoke up to remind me I had dropped the Miz. In bed with her I had not used her name at all. We were nameless that afternoon. But somehow the competition with another man for her affection had erased the Miz. When I got back to school I planned to ring her on the telephone, call her Bonny, and thank her and tell her what a good dancer she is. I'd tell her how much I'd like to go trail riding with her when I was back for the summer.

I didn't know what Gilwall was pushing for the US government in Central and South America that was so important that he'd leave a woman like that alone for very long. Maybe Gilwall thought saving the American Way was more important than saving his marriage. Maybe he didn't care? Maybe he knew she could and would take care of her needs herself. Saving us from communism was his gig, I guess.

Before reaching the highway heading northeast on the way back to school, I saw a tall lean black woman standing at the last bus stop in town. She was holding a purse in one hand, the other hand clasping the collar of her long coat, holding it tight around her neck. I pulled over to the curb and leaned out and said, "My girlfriend and I just broke up. Can I give you these flowers I'd gotten for her?"

The woman eyed me suspiciously for a moment. Then she said, "I'm sorry about your girlfriend. But I'm happy to have these flowers." She smiled at the bouquet of tulips as she took them in her hands. When she looked back at me, she said, "Don't worry Honey, you'll find another girlfriend." And she was right.

I pulled onto Rt 41 heading north. After a couple of miles I turned onto a country road and stopped the car. I sat there listening to the engine for a couple of minutes before I did a u-turn and headed for home.

In a drawer in my room I found my camera, a 35mm Argus I bought from Toby at the pawnshop. I needed something to take pictures of horses and girls. I hadn't taken it to school because I figured somebody would steal it even though we had the honor system. Somebody had told me to keep film in the refrigerator if you want it to last and I had stuck a few rolls in the back of the bottom shelf where Mom never bothered to look. A roll of 35 mm film was still there. So I loaded up and headed for Mr. Hamlyn's farm.

When I got to the farm, a survey crew was busy measuring and mapping and hammering stakes into the ground. I took a few pictures of the barn and the paddock, and a bunch of pictures of the big oak tree that shaded the office. It must have been about three hundred years old but it was in the way of progress.

I drove on up the road to the Elmendorf Orchards to take a few pictures there. I kind of regret going over there because a couple of bull dozers had half the orchard cleared and were growling at the rest of the trees that were just starting to bud out. But the heavy equipment hadn't gotten to the rows of apple trees where I had seen Lockett riding naked. I took a bunch of pictures from every angle. Maybe someday I'd find Lockett and show them to her. I've got a lot of stories to tell her, too. And let her know how my freethinking is going.

On the road to school I kept glancing at the camera on the seat beside me thinking how it held so many memories, even if they were all in black and white. The crazy thing is that somebody did steal the camera before I could even get the pictures developed. So I just have my own memories of Hamlyn's farm and Lockett's orchard. But they are in color and they stay right with me.

Acknowledgments

I am grateful to Sarah Boggs, Karen V. Kibler, and Nancy Cleary for their organizational contributions and to my wife, Gwen Cates, for her support, criticism, and her artistic contribution. I am also want to thank Diane DeBell for her ever keen-eyed wisdom.

I send a prayer of thanks to three special horses that taught me so much and carried me many miles: Rocco Rex, Thor, and Tantara.

CPSIA information can be obtained at www.ICGtesting.com
Printed in the USA
BVOW070107121011

273392BV00001B/1/P